Conned

CHARITY PARKERSON

Punk & Sissy

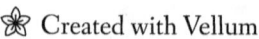 Created with Vellum

Introduction

FOUR MONTHS. COUNTLESS CALLS,
TEXTS, AND STEAMY NIGHTS. ALL
LIES.

All Army wants is to meet his biggest TV obsession, Tanner Murray. He's watched the man playing one of Primetime's sexiest vampires for years. When he learns his celebrity crush is appearing at a local comic con, Army doesn't waste any time getting his ticket. After getting lost, making a new friend, and standing in the world's longest line, Army gets one fan experience he'll never forget.

Tanner, A.K.A. Brit, meets men and women everywhere he goes. Being a celebrity means there's no shortage of willing bodies. The only difference between Army and the rest is that Army is the only person Tanner has ever slept with more than once.

That doesn't mean the man has him tied down, or that he knows Tanner at all.

After Army walks away from Tanner, he never expects to see the man again. In fact, he hopes he never will. The only thing Tanner has ever done for Army is break his heart. When circumstances land Tanner on Army's doorstep, Army vows this time things will be different. He has no idea how right he is.

Author Note

I hope this is the one and only time I have to give this type of back story on a book, but I'm doing so for a good cause. The original version of this story was just a short meet cute—no sex or even kissing. You see, I was contacted by someone representing a small publishing company, asking for a donated story for an anthology to raise money for cancer. I wrote a short piece around 3,000 words and sent it to them. A few weeks later, they contacted me again, saying the only way they would include my story was if my characters weren't gay, because the CEO of the publishing house is a Baptist. They said if I'd change my story to an M/F story, I could be included. In that moment, it no longer mattered if they'd be willing to accept me if I changed my story, because I was no longer willing to accept them. Refusing to accept a donation because a character is gay isn't faith. It's hate, and they obviously know nothing about me if they think for one minute I'll stand for that. I withdrew my submission and made it longer. Now, with all the sexy scenes and hot kisses included, Brit and Army's romance will help raise money for a different worthy cause—The Trevor Project, a charity that helps at-risk LGBT youth. A portion of this book's proceeds will go to support the only thing that spreads even faster than hate and fear—love.

Chapter One

"I AM COMPLETELY AND UTTERLY LOST." Army's words fell on deaf ears since he stood in an empty, endless hallway. Never in his life had Army been inside such a massive hotel before. It was like a tiny city. He'd already stopped two hotel employees and asked for directions. One had unhelpfully suggested he download an app to his phone that contained a map of the property. The second person he stopped handed him a paper map before pointing him in this direction. To a hall. An empty hall.

With a loud sigh, Army tucked the paper map beneath his arm and opened the app on his phone. Maybe between the two, he could figure out where he was supposed to be. If he missed his chance to get

Tanner Murray's autograph, Army would make this hotel's existence miserable. For sure they'd get a bad review on Yelp. A frustrated growl stayed lodged in his throat as he struggled to balance his autograph book and the map, and scroll through his phone. No matter how many times he pinched the screen before spreading his fingers wide, the image didn't enlarge.

"Are you looking for the Vamps in Space convention?"

A startled cry escaped Army at the question. The map floated to the floor as Army juggled his phone from hand to hand, attempting to stop it from going the way of the map. He finally managed to smack it to his chest and hold it there. His heart raced. Each rapid beat kissed the face of Army's phone as he held it tight against him, trying to calm himself. He sucked in a deep breath. The purple-haired girl who'd appeared from nowhere barely reached the center of his chest. With her chin tilted up and staring at him with heavily black-lined gray eyes, she waited for his answer.

Army sucked in another deep breath and pushed his glasses up his nose. "Um. Yeah. Sorry. I didn't see you there."

She flashed him a quick smile before returning to the alcove where she'd obviously been hiding. After unplugging a cord, she moved back to his side. "Sorry about that. I didn't mean to startle you. As big as this place is, they don't have many outlets. I had to charge my phone. So, are you lost?"

Army nodded, thankful not to be alone. "Yeah. I've been wandering around for half an hour, trying to find the convention. They gave me a map, but it's pretty much useless as far as I can tell."

She nodded. "I had the same problem last year when they moved from the convention center downtown to here. This place is huge and they have way too much going on at the same time. I'm headed that way if you're interested."

Relief rushed through Army. A smile tugged at his lips. "Thanks. I'd like that."

She shrugged and went back to donning an unaffected mask. Since he'd dealt with his share of goth girls, Army wasn't insulted. He assumed it was part of the initiation or an oath they took. Whatever. Either way, none of them ever smiled. "It's no big deal," she said as they fell into step beside each other.

"Tanner Murray is signing autographs next, and he's on my list, so I was headed that way."

He was on Army's list too, but he didn't think they meant it the same way. "That's who I was headed to see. I was afraid I wouldn't find the convention in time."

Falling out of character once more, the girl smiled. "You're a Tanner Murray fan? He's amazing. I know he isn't on the show any longer, but he's still my favorite. Did you sign the petition that went around, demanding he be brought back?" Before he could answer, she held her hand out for him. "I'm Jaylah, by the way."

"Army," Army said, accepting her handshake.

"Oh, like the actor."

Army nodded. "Except spelled differently, and yeah, I signed. I hope they bring him back. The show hasn't been the same since they killed him off. I mean, I'll keep watching, but it hasn't been the same."

"Right?" Jaylah said.

They rounded a corner, taking a left where he'd taken a right earlier, and found the crowd. He spotted a sign hanging from the ceiling with Tanner's name listed, but he couldn't see the man's table. The mob of people surrounding him was too thick.

"Whoa. Is that the line already? It doesn't start for fifteen more minutes."

Jaylah nodded. "The whole convention has been like this."

Army held his silence. He hated admitting he was only there for Tanner. He was a fan of the show, but he wasn't insane over it. Army knew from checking the website that some of the best tickets were five thousand apiece and those had sold out fifteen minutes after going live. He couldn't imagine being that big of a fan. Of course, he had no right to judge. This was his fourth convention, in four different states. He was a huge fan... of Tanner.

"We'd better get in line," Jaylah said, rushing ahead. He fought to keep up, but she snagged a spot and waved him over. Jaylah went up onto her toes as if trying to spot Tanner. Army swallowed down a laugh. If he couldn't see the front, being almost two feet taller than her, Jaylah didn't stand a chance.

"It's long," Army said, hating to burst her bubble. They moved forward a good ten feet. "But it looks like it's moving," he added, trying to hide his excitement.

She turned and focused on him, looking intense. "Be honest. How do I look?"

Since it was obvious this meant a lot to her, Army took his time inspecting her from head to foot. "Everything seems in place."

With a sharp nod, Jaylah faced forward again, trying one more time to see over the crowd. "Can you see him yet?"

He knew they hadn't moved enough for anything to change, but Army checked anyhow. "No. I'll let you know."

Her shoulders fell as she focused on him once more. "You must think I'm an idiot. I mean, it's not like Tanner Murray will take one look at me and fall in love. It's just the principle of it, you know?"

Even though they'd just met, loyalty had Army nodding. "I get it."

She tried one more time seeing above everyone. "Grrr. I hate being short. My ex, Jay, he's six-foot-eight and we've always done these things together, but we broke up six months ago, and now I can't see anything."

"Jay and Jaylah. That's cute." It was, but Army had hit the point of merely making conversation. He was ready to get to the front of the line.

"I used to think so," she said, sounding absent. "Then he won a trip for two to Vamp Camp in L.A. and took my best friend Chrissy instead of me."

Army tore his gaze away from the crowd surrounding Tanner's table to focus on Jaylah. "That's awful."

Her gray eyes looked sad. "Yeah, but don't worry. My friend Will is a level eight mage. He cast a spell to give them herpes."

Against his will, Army was sucked into the story. "Is Will's magic reliable?"

"Meh," Jaylah said with a shrug. "But Will is Chrissy's ex-boyfriend, and I'm banking he already gave her herpes and knew where it was headed next."

Army's eyebrows rose. He fought not to laugh. "Good thing you're over it."

"Right?" she said, sounding relieved.

He focused ahead again. Two people standing at the edge of the autograph table shifted, giving Army a clear view of Tanner. The breath caught in Army's throat. "I see him," Army said, hearing the excitement in his voice, and incapable of hiding it.

"How close are we? What's he wearing? Does he look as amazing in person?"

"About twenty more people ahead of us. He's wearing his outfit from the show. You know, leather jacket, white shirt, and jeans. He looks even better in person."

Jaylah bounced in place. Excitement filled her gaze when she focused on him. "What should I say when I get up there?"

Army shrugged. "I don't even know what I'll say."

"I'm asking for a hug," Jaylah shot back, proving she'd already had a plan in place. Before he could call her on it, she asked, "So why are you here alone?"

His gaze skirted away. "I do everything alone." The crowd moved forward another ten feet as he made the admission.

"That's sad."

"Not really," Army said with a shrug. "I like being by myself."

"Still," Jaylah said, not letting it go. "You have great hair and really pretty blue eyes. Even your glasses can't hide your good looks. It doesn't make sense for someone like you to be alone."

He wasn't entirely sure what his hair and eyes had to do with anything, but Army still took the compliment. "Thank you. I—" The people in front of them moved aside, making him realize Jaylah was next, and killing the words in his throat.

Tanner's blond hair was perfect and looked soft. Everything about the man was amazing, from his straight white teeth to his light-blue eyes. Those gorgeous eyes remained locked on Jaylah. "Hi. Did you have something you needed signed?"

Without a word, Jaylah shoved her autograph book beneath the man's nose. It was obvious she'd frozen, forgetting about her hug beneath the gorgeous man's stare.

Tanner bent his head over the book and signed his name. There was nothing personal about the moment. In the man's defense, Jaylah hadn't even given her name.

"You look hot." Horror raced through Army as Tanner's gaze slid his way at the asinine comment.

"Thank you."

Heat exploded through Army's face. He didn't even know where the words had come from. They'd popped from his mouth without a thought. "I meant temperature wise," Army explained. "With that leather coat on," he tacked on, because he couldn't stop. Army could feel Jaylah's stare boring into the side of his face, but he didn't turn his head. He couldn't stop staring into Tanner's eyes. "I mean, it's cold outside, but not in here." Why couldn't he stop?

The humor in Tanner's gaze deepened. "You're right." The man stood and peeled off his jacket. The move had the man's t-shirt stretching tight across his hard muscles. Army's mouth went dry. "You should hang on to this for me," Tanner added. He handed it Army's way.

Army's fingers automatically closed around the leather piece. It was heavier than he expected. The star's cologne engulfed him, making Army's stomach growl. Army glanced down at the material, speechless.

"What's your name?" Tanner asked.

"Army," Army's mouth answered with no help from his brain.

Tanner glanced past Army, eyeing the line. "It should take about thirty more minutes to get through this line. They've blocked off the second floor for me. If you head up that way, I'll meet you then and get my coat back. Until then, keep it safe."

Without thought, Army clutched it to his chest and nodded. He walked away without waiting for his autograph. He had the man's coat and plans to see him in half an hour. That was so much better.

Jaylah stood waiting for him, all pretense of goth-hood gone. Her mouth hung open. "Oh my gosh. You are now my best friend in the whole world. What just happened? I was standing there and even I don't know what happened. You should've told him he looked overheated in his pants."

"If I'd known he would strip, I would have," Army said, incapable of keeping the excitement from his voice. He brought the coat to his nose. It smelled like heaven, leather, and man.

"I've never been more jealous of anyone in my life. If you don't text me afterward and tell me what happened, I'll never forgive you."

A hint of panic wormed its way in. He couldn't tell her that. Army made a mental note to remember to forget to ask for her number. "He said half an hour," Army reminded her. "Do you know where the nearest elevator is? I'm too excited to wait."

She pointed down the hall. "There's one down there on the right. Come find me later," she demanded.

He nodded. "Will do."

With one final conspiratorial smile, Army headed for the elevator. It was a short ride up from the first floor to the second. Still, he could barely stand still. The leather material never left his nose. Excitement had his stomach dancing, and his heart turned cartwheels in his chest. When the door slid open, two large security men blocked his path. They took one look at him and stepped aside. Army didn't make eye contact as he passed. Spotting a set of plush white chairs, Army made a beeline for them. He didn't know how much time had passed, but it felt like hours. Would he show? There was always the chance Tanner would send his personal assistant to retrieve the jacket and Army would spend the rest of the convention hiding from Jaylah. Tanner didn't have to keep his word to meet him. Once that thought settled in, Army's nerves frayed to the point of breakage. He almost stood and walked away. Instead, he buried his nose in the jacket once more and inhaled, drawing strength from the other man's scent.

A set of warm lips brushed the back of his neck, causing goosebumps to break out across Army's skin. "You're showing up more and more often at these events."

The smile tugging at the corners of Army's mouth was out of his control. "You're getting worse and worse at hiding me."

Those gorgeous soft lips he'd felt against his skin in the last four states he'd visited now brushed against Army's nape once more. "Maybe I don't care to hide you." Before Army had time to let those words sink in, Tanner straightened away. "Would you like a tour of my room? It's beautiful."

Army stood and accepted Tanner's outstretched hand, allowing the man to pull him along. He was ready to go anywhere the man led. Four conventions. Four months. Endless texts and calls. Throughout it all, Army still hadn't awoken from the dream of being the center of Tanner's attention. In fact, Tanner trusted him enough to admit that all his real friends called him Brit. He refused to let Army call him anything else. Army didn't know how long this would last, but he was holding on until the end.

Brit's gaze followed Army's every move as the man trailed from one room to the next, inspecting Brit's enormous hotel suite. One of the many reasons this year's vampire convention had been moved to this hotel was due to their ability to handle multiple celebrity visitors, keeping them safe from the influx of crazed fans. No matter the reasons, Brit loved watching Army as he tried hiding his thoughts. Army wasn't impressed, but he obviously didn't want to insult Brit. When he looked around, his faked expressions didn't fool Brit. Army couldn't care less about the expensive furnishings. When the man's gaze landed on Brit, his face lit with genuine excitement. Maybe that was why Brit couldn't stay away. Fuck it. He wouldn't kid himself. The way Army's eyes lit was exactly why Brit kept inviting Army back. Before Army, Brit hadn't slept with the same person twice in years. This man, though, there was something about him. He wanted Brit, but Brit didn't think it was because he was famous. Army wanted him for some reason all his own. Brit needed to know.

"This place is gorgeous. Just not as much as you," Army added. It was funny how Army's tone hadn't changed—like he spoke of the weather. Yet Brit's body reacted as if the most sultry of words had been spoken against his neck.

"Three days is too long without you."

A slow smile stretched Army's lips. "I'm a librarian. Traveling as much as you do is out of my reach. I'm trying to come to you as often as I can."

Brit nodded. "I know, and I'm trying to come to you as often as I can. That still doesn't change the fact that three days is too long without you. Who was your friend downstairs?" Brit asked, changing the subject before he jumped Army and all chance at conversation was lost.

Army moved closer to Brit. "Jaylah. We met about an hour ago. You're changing the subject."

It wasn't like Brit could call him a liar. "You should take up acting. Your reaction to me handing you my jacket was priceless."

The distance between them disappeared. Army pressed against him. Their matched heights had them nose to nose. Brit loved the man's blue eyes. He was gorgeous. "I wasn't acting. Having any part of you is like a dream come true. You're right. Three days is too long."

Brit broke. His lips found Army's like opposite ends of a magnet. The shirt he wore pulled tight against his back as Army tightened his hold on the material. It was a dangerous game he played with Army. Brit was wrong to spend so much time with the man. He hadn't thought anyone could get to him. Brit also hadn't anticipated Army's kiss. Army kissed like he'd taken a fucking class on the subject. He hesitated at just the right moments, drawing Brit in before sucking Brit's bottom lip. Everything was perfectly timed with the precise pressure and skill to rock Brit to his core. Army made Brit forget a world existed outside of them.

Army loosened the button on Brit's jeans.

Brit's breath caught. If there was anything Army did better than kiss, it was the way he fucked. Jesus. The man was an addiction.

Army's lips moved from Brit's mouth to his jaw. Cool air brushed his hips as Army dragged the material lower. Brit's hands never moved from holding Army's jaw. It wasn't that he didn't want to touch Army everywhere. Army made him useless. Brit had no clue why Army came back for more. He had to be the most boring fuck Army ever had. When Army touched him, Brit surrendered.

Army cupped Brit's erection through his underwear. "You mess with my head. The way your cock leaks like you're dying for me is the biggest high. Damn, I must've been very good in a past life."

Brit tilted his chin up and gave Army better access to his throat. Army licked his pulse once more before pulling away long enough to steal Brit's shirt. He threw his off too, making Brit whimper when their bare chests met. Through a haze of lust, Brit struggled for air and watched as Army calmly removed his glasses. He set them on the nearby table. Their gazes met. Army didn't look away as he slid Brit's underwear down his hips. He walked backward, holding Brit's stare. A condom appeared between the man's fingers. He bit the corner and ripped the package open. Brit couldn't look away as Army set his erection free and rolled the condom down his length. Brit kicked out of his clothes and followed. Army sat on the couch. Brit didn't need verbal instructions. He obeyed Army's silent commands. The man held him hostage with his intense blue stare. Brit straddled Army. A cry of relief ripped from his throat as Army's cock filled him. Brit didn't know how one person could feel so goddamn empty without another person around, but he was there with Army. He let those thoughts fall away as he rocked himself on Army's dick. Army watched him as if studying his every reaction and adjusting his pace to Brit's needs.

"Tell me nice things," Army demanded.

Brit couldn't think straight. His body burned with desire.

Army reached between them and jacked Brit's dick. "You mean you don't have a single good thing to say?"

Brit had no idea how Army managed to appear so unaffected while Brit thought his mind might snap. He wasn't sure he could still formulate words, much less a thought. "Bloody, hell, Army. You're killing me."

The man's smirk only managed to set Brit on fire even more than he already was. "That's it, Brit. Use that sexy accent against me." Army's eyes fell closed for a second, as if the pleasure was too much. "God-damn, sexy. You're amazing." His hips lifted as he pumped inside Brit. "I could stay inside you forever. You're so hot and tight. Perfect."

Brit's cock leaked on Army's stomach. He dropped his head to Army's shoulder and stared down at the mess. With a tight grip on the back of the couch, Brit took his pleasure from Army. He was so fucking close. The air felt devoid of oxygen. He couldn't catch his breath. The ecstasy Army promised was just out of reach. Brit wanted the orgasm only Army could give him, but he equally didn't want the moment to end. The only time he felt like anything other than a puppet was when Army set him free. In Army's arms, he was just Brit—real and raw.

Army's long fingers encircled Brit's soaked dick. Brit's lips parted on a pant. The sight was more erotic than the raunchiest of porn. Then Army stroked, squeezing near the tip, and swiped his thumb across Brit's crown. The thin floodgates holding back his insanity snapped. A cry tore from his lips. His teeth sank into Army's shoulder as he tried hanging on to reality. He couldn't breathe past the bliss choking him.

"Jesus, Brit. I don't know how to stay away," Army admitted as he continued pumping inside Brit. He pulled Brit's hair, forcing his mouth to Army's. Brit's bottom lip stung as Army's teeth sank into his flesh. He moaned around Brit's tongue as his orgasm hit. Brit wanted to beat his chest. Army made him feel like he was invincible. Their kiss softened as the fire simmered to a warmth. As always, the moment the insanity passed, the guilt set in. Army didn't know him. Not really. If he did, he'd despise Brit. He could never, ever let Army find out the truth about him. Brit couldn't lose this connection. The problem was, the more Army came around, the bigger the risk. Brit shifted, kissing Army's jaw before pressing light kisses against the man's ear and throat. There had to be a middle ground. Surely there was a way he could keep Army and not lose everything else.

THE LARGE HOTEL suite felt way too big without Brit's larger-than-life personality filling it. Army found himself trailing from room to room and back again. The entire place smelled like Brit. Too many times to count, Army forced himself to rearrange his features to temper his out-of-control smile. The only time he felt like this was with Brit. He didn't know how to stop coming around. In the past four months, he'd shown up four times. It would've been more if Army could afford it, but as it was, he could only attend the conventions closest his home state. Even then, the expense was killing him. Luckily, Brit didn't have any problem turning up at Army's door.

Between those visits, their countless Facetime visits, texts, calls, and every other way they could think to be together, Brit had completely stolen Army. He knew he was sick with love and want. The problem was, so was half the rest of the population. What real shot did Army have?

The convention raged on without Army. He could've gone out and enjoyed the fun while Brit finished his appearances and panels. Instead, he chose to ramble around and pine. A huge grin spread across his face again, forcing Army to rearrange his features once more. He also didn't want to run into Jaylah. She would want a story. The truth was for Brit and him alone.

Army paused at the edge of the bed. He could strip and wait, but that seemed desperate, even to him. His cheeks ached, making him realize how big his smile had grown again. Jesus, he had a problem. The sound of someone banging around in the outer room had Army headed for the door. He couldn't get back to Brit fast enough. This time, Army didn't try beating back his grin. Brit had obviously knocked over a footstool. He was bent, straightening the furniture. Army enjoyed the view. Damn, everything about the sexy actor was hotter than hell.

"Now, that's a gorgeous sight."

Brit spun and startled slightly at the sight of Army—like he'd forgotten Army was there. "Hey." Brit's voice was deeper than usual, as if his throat hurt from talking too much.

"Hey, to you, too. I didn't expect you back for at least another hour. Panels usually run longer." Army eyed Brit's outfit. He'd been wearing a t-shirt and jeans when he'd left. Now he sported some crazy ninja costume that covered him from head to toe, including his head and face. Only the man's gorgeous blue eyes were visible. "What are you wearing?"

"It's for my latest movie."

Despite the oddness of Brit's costume, Army was still turned on. Damn, Brit made everything sexy. He sidled closer to the sexy man of his dreams. "When did you change?" He eyed Brit's odd ninja-style shoes. "And what kind of shoes are you wearing?"

A line appeared between Brit's eyes, as if confused by Army's questions. His gaze dropped to Army's feet before slowly coming back to rest on Army's face. "What did you say your name was again?"

Army blinked. He looked closer at Brit. The man's eyes were dilated to the point Army could barely tell their color, and he hardly blinked. Army stopped breathing. He knew that look too well. He'd grown up with a junkie. "It's Army. What are you on?"

One corner of Brit's mouth lifted in a smirk. "Like the actor."

Army tried taking a breath, but it hurt. His eyes stung. "Yeah, except it's spelled differently. What did you take?" he asked again. Damn, Brit couldn't even remember his name, or that they'd had this conversation before.

Brit dug a prescription bottle from his pocket. He shook it at Army, but Army couldn't read the label. "You want some? God knows, there's no shortage of doctors willing to write me whatever prescription I need."

"No, thank you," Army said through clenched teeth and crippling pain. "I think I'll head back home."

"What's the rush?" Brit asked as he closed the space between them. He wrapped his arms around Army and grabbed two handfuls of ass before hauling Army against him. There was no missing the erection between them. And, fuck, it was like Brit's muscles were twice as big. Army didn't like the sudden disadvantage. Brit never manhandled him. "You should stay and take care of me. Surely you don't want to leave me in this condition."

"If you can still get it up as high as you are, you're capable of taking care of yourself."

Brit shoved him away. "Why did you let me fuck you the first place if you plan to get pious now?" Brit didn't give him time to answer. "You fucked me because I'm some vampire you saw on TV and crushed on, that's why. You don't know me. Nor do you want to. You like the idea of fucking a celebrity. The excitement of it all. Well, here I am, Army. I'm offering you all the thrills you'll ever need."

Army ground his back teeth. He didn't know what was going on, but he didn't like this version of Brit. He never would've messed with the man if he'd known about the drugs. It had been a long time since Army hated himself. If Brit knew him at all, he wouldn't have pulled this shit with Army here. "What about you?" Army asked, taking even himself by surprise with his deadly tone. "What do you know about me?"

"Not a goddamn thing," Brit answered without an ounce of shame in his voice. Not that the man was capable of feeling much at the moment, Army was sure. "I don't want to know you. Tomorrow, you'll be gone, and I'll move to the next town, where there'll be another one of you waiting."

"No."

Brit's eyebrows hit his hairline at Army's denial. "Oh, I promise you, there'll be another."

Army shook his head. "Maybe, but I won't be gone tomorrow. I'll be gone tonight." He headed for the door, intent on making good on his threat.

Brit blocked his path, moving faster than Army thought possible, considering his high. "If you walk out now, don't come crawling back."

Rage had Army firing back. "Do you have any idea how ridiculous you sound right now? You think I want to see you again? That's rich." Army slammed the door closed behind him with more force than intended. In a matter of hours, his life had gone from the highest of highs to the lowest of lows. He should've known better. The minute they'd met, Army had known the man was too good to be true.

Not to mention, nothing good ever happened to Army. Why should this be any different? When Army reached his car, a snort escaped him. It was an ugly sound, echoing through the parking garage. The fact that he'd found his way around the hotel with ease while leaving Brit, when it had been hard as hell to find the man, was all the sign Army needed. He shouldn't have come here. He was also a goddamn idiot who would never have anything.

Army climbed behind the wheel and crammed his keys in the ignition. The rage bled from him, leaving him deflated. He glanced up. The mirror on the back of the sun visor met him. His reflection stared back at him. Army looked every bit as ripped to shreds as he felt. Right now, anger saved him from falling apart. But he already knew it would be short lived. The moment his temper cooled, pain would be waiting. Right or not. Ridiculous or not, Army had fallen for Brit. It was over. They were done. Chances were good that Brit would never think of him again. He was no one. Just as Brit had assured him.

Chapter Two

To ANYONE ELSE, it might seem a ridiculous waste of time to run home on his lunch break to grab his forgotten lunch. Unfortunately, Army's tall frame required nourishment to keep moving. On paper, being a librarian didn't sound taxing. In reality, there was a lot of walking and lifting involved. Plus, since coming home from the convention, Army's mood had been complete shit. When he went hungry, he was twice the asshole. The two things combined meant ugly things for his co-workers and patrons. No one deserved that. He was saving everyone from himself.

A plain black sedan sat in the driveway of Army's two-bedroom cabin-style home. Damn, he hoped it wasn't someone serving him with court papers. He thought he had all the collection agencies held at bay, but who knew. There might still be someone out there he didn't know about. His mom had fucked up his credit and life beyond all repair. Things kept hitting him from left field. Army had never been more tired in his life and there wasn't an ounce of hope in sight, much less a light at the end of the tunnel.

He parked in the grass beside the car, leaving room for the vehicle to get out of the driveway around him. Even though the windows were tinted, he could see there wasn't anyone inside. With a final deep breath, Army headed for the door. When he caught sight of the black clad figure, dressed in a stocking cap and sunglasses, sitting on his front steps, Army almost turned around. He only had so long for lunch. There weren't enough hours in the day to deal with Brit. It had only been a week since the last time he'd set eyes on the man. Damned if it didn't feel like an eternity. There was no excuse for how his heart skipped a beat at the first sight of him.

"Hey," Brit said, sounding every bit as unsure of his welcome as he should.

Army swallowed around the hurt and anger. "Hey."

Brit came to his feet. "I couldn't stay away." He didn't sound happy about it.

"You should have."

"Okay. Ouch," Brit said in the driest tone Army had ever heard.

Army rocked back on his heels and buried his hands in his coat pockets. "Seriously, Brit. You shouldn't be surprised. You made it clear I don't mean anything to you."

"I need a favor," Brit said before Army could work himself up.

An ugly-sounding snort escaped Army. He pushed his way past Brit and shoved his key in the door. "Of course, you do. Every fucking junkie in the world needs something from me. That's why my life is a fucking mess. You may as well join the team." He was too pissed off to tell Brit to fuck off. The man followed him inside. His phone was ringing. Army raced to answer while doing his best to ignore Brit's presence.

"Hello?" Even to Army's ears, he sounded winded.

"May I speak to Army Nelson?"

Army pinched the bridge of his nose. He recognized the nasally voice of the woman who worked for the company that financed his car. "This is he."

"Mr. Nelson, are you aware you are forty-five days late on your car payment?"

"Yes, I'm aware. I spoke to you last week, and you extended my grace period. As far as I'm aware, that deal still holds." Fuck. Of course this would happen while Brit stared at him. Life did enjoy kicking him around.

"It's company policy to do a follow-up to ensure you intend to you hold up your end. Can we still expect payment by Friday?"

Army nodded, even though she couldn't see him. "Yes. I get paid on Friday. I'll pay online after my direct deposit goes through."

"Okay. Let me give you my name, number, and the extension where I can be reached, in case you run into any snags."

Army grabbed a nearby pen and scratch pad. "Sounds good." He scratched out the woman's information while avoiding Brit's gaze. Brit probably hadn't been late paying a bill in his life. In fact, he probably had someone who handled all this on his behalf. With his phone call at an end, and nothing else to hold his attention, Army had no other choice than to focus on Brit.

Brit watched him with knowing eyes. Army's chest hurt. Losing Brit hurt bad enough without this added punishment. "You should've said something."

With a shrug, Army glanced away. "Like what? My mom stole my identity shortly before she did all the heroin and ended up dead, leaving me the biggest mess imaginable? Exactly when would I have sneaked that in?"

The pity in Brit's expression was worse than a hot iron poker through the eye. Brit sat on the arm of the couch. "I have a proposition for you."

Army puffed out his cheeks and rubbed the back of his neck. Would this day ever end? "I'm listening."

"I didn't show up today on a whim. Apparently, you weren't the only bridge I burned during my lapse last week."

An ugly snort escaped Army. "Your lapse," he said, repeating Brit's words.

"I can be an ass."

"You don't say," Army said, incapable of not being a dick about it.

"I need a place to stay while the bad press dies down," Brit said, powering through in spite of Army's attitude.

Army grabbed his forgotten lunch from the fridge. If only he hadn't left it behind this morning, he might've missed Brit and this awful conversation. "Good luck with that."

Brit didn't give up. "No one knows about us."

"Big surprise," Army said, taking a bite of his sandwich. He still had to eat his lunch if he hoped to survive the day.

"I'd hoped you'd let me stay here until someone else fucks up and takes my spot in the news."

Army swallowed his bite before he choked. Still, he couldn't avoid a coughing fit. He turned up a bottle of water before he died. "You've got to be fucking kidding me," Army said, wiping his mouth. "I've never met anyone with more nerve."

"I'll pay you twenty-five-thousand dollars to let me crash here and to keep quiet about me being here."

Brit was serious. It was written in the way he held his head high. Army couldn't look away. "I don't want your money." Because, fuck him. Brit thought he could waltz in here and buy Army because he had financial problems.

"You need help," Brit argued.

That was it. "Get out."

Brit didn't budge. "It's partially my fault," Brit said, digging deeper. "I've expected you to meet me at conventions all over the place. It wasn't fair, and you didn't deserve to have me plague your life."

"Where will you go if I stand by my earlier no?" He fucking hated that he cared.

"I don't know." The sincerity in Brit's tone had Army ready to curse a blue streak.

He checked his watch. If he left right this second, he'd still be at least five minutes late getting back to work. He glanced around, seeking answers he didn't have. Giving in, he snagged his spare key from where it hung on the wall. Army passed it Brit's way. "You can stay, for now. I have to get back to work. You can sleep on the couch." He held Brit's gaze, needing the man to know how serious he was. "Three things," he said, holding up three fingers and ticking them off as he went. "Don't steal my stuff. It's not worth anything, but it's all I have. Don't fucking touch me because we are so over it's ridiculous. And, I don't want your money."

Brit nodded, but he didn't do a good job of hiding his hurt. "I'm sorry for whatever I said to drive you away."

"You don't remember?" Army didn't know which was worse: Brit recalling every hateful word or the man not even knowing how he'd broken Army.

Brit shook his head. "I just know you stormed out, and I hadn't heard from you until I turned up here. It must've been bad."

The way Brit watched him tugged at Army's heart. He didn't want to be moved. Fuck. Why did it have to be this man? No one else got to him. "You made it clear I wasn't anyone to you other than a fuck. I was just one person in a long line of men you could and would have the second I was gone."

Brit's eyes fell closed for a second before he focused on Army once more. "I didn't mean it."

"Addicts rarely mean anything they say," Army shot back. "But that doesn't change a thing."

"I'm not an addict."

Army scrubbed his hands through his hair. Brit drove him insane. "Yeah. That's the same thing my mom always said right before I ended up in a new foster home. Forgive me if I've gotten too old to swallow that bullshit."

He hated Brit's sad expression. "I don't know how to prove myself to you."

Army shrugged. "Maybe you can't, but it doesn't really matter, because I don't want to love anyone else who loves drugs more than me."

"Is that a fear? That you'll fall for me," Brit clarified.

No matter how hard he tried, Army's voice wouldn't work. He shrugged again and shook his head. No way would he admit it was too late. Those four months Brit had given him had ruined Army for anyone else. But—like he'd said—it didn't matter. In the end, love wouldn't make Brit clean.

Brit stared at some point past Army. "I think it's too late for me," he said, sounding like it was more for himself than Army. "You're already the first thought in my head every morning." With that punch to the gut still hanging between them, Brit shoved the key to Army's house in his front pocket. "If you won't take my money, at least let me make sure you have something waiting for you to eat when you get home."

Army shrugged and headed for the door. "Whatever. I get home around six. Don't make me sorry." He slipped outside and slammed the door behind him without giving Brit time to respond. Since he was already sorry, there was nothing Brit could say anyway.

BRIT STARED at the spot where Army had been. When the door didn't fly back open, and Army didn't take his words back, Brit bent at the waist and sucked air. There was no way he could've prepared for Army's hatred. It was worse than a thousand knives through the heart. He'd expected it to be bad, but nothing could've prepared him for Army's anger. There was no describing what it was like to go from being in the man's loving arms to staring into the man's sexy eyes filled with hatred.

There had to be some way to make things up to him. He could've gone anywhere in the world to hide out. There was only one place he wanted to be. Brit's gaze landed on the notes Army scratched out from his phone call. It didn't take a genius to figure out Army had money issues. That was one problem Brit could make go away. Even if Army couldn't forgive him, Brit wanted Army to be happy. Fuck. Army claimed Brit had told him he was only one man in a long line of many. Brit didn't doubt it for a second. Bugger. He didn't know how to come back from that. Army planned to pay his car note online. Brit's gaze slid to the open laptop on the kitchen counter. He slid his finger across the laptop's pointing device, bringing the computer to life. He typed in the name of the finance company. The name auto-filled after two letters. That was good. When the homepage popped up, the man's username and password automatically filled in. A smile that felt evil even to him stretched Brit's lips. He logged in and checked the balance. It wasn't that bad. Even though he knew the payoff would be less than the full balance, he liked the thought of Army getting a surprise check for the amount he'd overpaid. In a matter of a few clicks, Army owned his car. A small slice of guilt lifted from his shoulders. He'd done something to make Army's life better. He hadn't completely ruined the man.

With that out of the way, Brit wandered the house, giving himself a tour. Every time he'd been there in the past, he'd seen the bedroom and nothing else. He'd always been in a hurry, rushing to see Army before needing to return to his tour. Now he noticed things he never had before. The living room was small, but the whole house was too. His couch was dark brown and looked to be some sort of microfiber. The entertainment center and coffee table were oak-colored, but Brit suspected they weren't real wood. Everything was clean—like meticulously so. How had he never noticed that about Army? Brit made his way down the short hallway. There were only two doors. The first led to a bathroom. It looked like it was never used. Brit could attest he'd never been in there before. There was nothing personal about the room and the cabinets were empty. Brit hit the other doorway. It was a library or reading room of sorts. Hell, maybe it was just where Army kept his massive number of books. There were bookcases next to bookcases, filled with books and nothing else. A smile tugged Brit's lips as he checked some of the titles. There was everything from classics to modern science fiction mixed with romance and history. Brit backed out of the room and headed back for the living room. There was one more doorway on the opposite side of the living room.

Brit bit his bottom lip as he crossed the threshold into what he knew to be Army's bedroom. He loved Army's large bed for so many reasons. When a person was tall like they were, it was impossible to sleep on a small mattress. The two of them together, they'd burned up the sheets. The bed was covered in a dark gray comforter. It was made, making Brit wonder if Army was a bit of clean freak. For a man who lived alone, his house seemed unnaturally at rights. Everything seemed to have its place. Once again, all the furniture was oak-colored, but not real wood. Brit opened the closet. Everything was perfect in there too. With a shake of his head, he closed the door and inspected the small bathroom inside the bedroom. Even though he'd been inside it before, Brit still looked at the tiny bathroom, as if it was the first time he'd seen it. The room only had a shower, toilet, and sink. Brit opened the cabinet above the sink. A smile touched his lips. This was the bathroom Army always used. There was toothpaste and aftershave. The shower had shampoo and body wash. This was Army's space. Brit's smile grew as he headed for the door. He needed to grab his bag from his rental. He was about to invade the hell out of Army's space. By the time Brit was through, Army wouldn't know what hit him, and he'd forget all about the convention.

"Sorry I'm late," Army said as he clocked back in after lunch.

"Did you meet a hot guy and get distracted?" Linda asked, laughing.

Army tossed a wink her way. "Nope. A sexy man showed up on my doorstep and offered me twenty-five-thousand dollars to let him stay with me for a while."

Linda snorted. She covered her mouth and nose when the sound came out louder than she'd obviously anticipated. "You're a riot. If you're not writing these crazy fantasies down for a book, I'm about to start. You could make a killing with your imagination. Does this sexy man have a name?"

"Brit," Army answered without a hint of shame. It wasn't as if Linda would ever believe him anyhow.

"Is that his real name, or do people call him that because he has a British accent?"

Her question gave him pause. Army had never thought to ask. After all, lots of actors used a stage name. Tanner could be his, but Brit did have a British accent. Of course, it didn't make sense for anyone to call the man by a nickname if he already had a stage name. Fuck, Army managed to confuse himself. "No," Army said, coming to a decision. "That's his real name, but he does have a British accent."

"Wow," Linda said, her voice taking on a dreamy edge. "I need a description."

Army grabbed a wheeled cart and started loading up the book returns. "My height. Blond hair and light-blue eyes. He's my age but looks even younger."

"The kind of man who will always look ten years less than his real age," Linda supplied.

Army nodded. "Exactly. His hair curls at the ends. When he wears a stocking cap, it curls around the edges, making him look like an angel." For a moment, Army got lost in the images in his head. Finally, the silence penetrated his daydreams. He turned to find Linda staring into space with a book held against her chest.

She blinked, coming back to herself when she realized Army was staring at her. "I miss being young," she said with a sad smile. She visibly shook off her melancholy and winked. "At the very least, I wish I had what it takes to be a bona fide cougar."

"You should do it," Army said, wishing Linda would. It could only liven up the place.

A blush touched her cheeks, and she waved his idea away. "Nah. I miss kissing, but I don't have what it takes to keep up with the kinky world we live in these days."

"No whips and chains for you, huh?"

Rather than laughing, as he expected, Linda looked thoughtful. "Hmmm," she hummed. She shook her head. "I guess I've never really considered it."

A surprised laugh escaped Army. "I'd better get these put away," he said, aiming the cart toward the shelves. "If I hang around too long, I'll have you signing up for one of those fetish lifestyles dating apps." He walked away, chuckling. If Linda decided she could be a cougar after all, maybe it would stop him from always telling all his secrets. Not that anyone believed him.

The light pouring in from the windows lessened as Army got lost in his work. He loved books. When he'd gotten hired at the library, he'd worried working with them every day would kill his fondness for reading. If anything, his love had grown. He couldn't count the number of times he brought pages to his nose and lost himself in the scent of their hidden dreams. Stories were so much better than reality, or at least they were better than his reality.

"Hey, Army."

Army startled at the sound of his name. He'd gotten lost in the silence and comfort of the building. He turned a smile Linda's way. "Yep?"

"Can I buy you dinner tonight? You know my sister is in town, and two weeks is just too much in each other's company. I need a night away."

As Army listened to Linda ramble, he pictured Brit at home with dinner waiting. The warmth in his chest hurt more than he anticipated. He had to be the most ridiculous person on the planet, falling in love with someone like Brit. Not only was the man out of his reach, he was everything Army had been trying to escape when he'd moved to the tiny town of Charlestown. Nothing exciting ever happened here, especially not drug-addicted boyfriends who broke hearts.

"I'd love to," Army said, interrupting Linda's long explanation.

"Yay," she cheered. Her smile made his acceptance worthwhile. At forty-two, Linda had given up on men, and Army genuinely liked her. He'd worried when he'd moved here that a small town would equal small minds. Linda had been the first person he'd met. She'd set his every fear to rest. In fact, she was closer to being a mother to him than his mother had ever been. If she needed an escape from her sister, he was there.

Brit shouldn't have been surprised when Army didn't turn up by six. Of course, he'd also never expected to find an enraged Army when he'd shown up on the man's doorstep. Brit wrapped his coat tighter around himself and shifted in the rocker on the porch, so he could kick his heels up onto the railing. His life was a fucked-up mess. He'd like to claim he didn't know exactly when that had happened, but he could point to the date on a calendar if asked. Army had become a beacon of hope for him, making him believe one day he'd have a real life. Now everything was fucked, and the man wasn't even coming home.

Charlestown was close enough to the beach and far enough south that it didn't drop to freezing in the winter, but it got cold enough to need a thick layer at night. Brit could go inside. Then again, he couldn't. Army was out there somewhere, thinking the worst of him. He'd racked his brain, trying to think of a way to explain. Brit's hands were tied. All he could do was hope—with enough time—he could prove himself. It wouldn't happen if Army kept avoiding him.

A set of headlights finally turned down the drive. Brit fought to keep his unaffected pose. It got harder when Army's tall form spilled from the car. Brit balled his hands into fists. He wanted to come to his feet and greet Army with a kiss. The temptation was choking. Instead, he stayed put. There was no stopping his eyes from eating Army alive. Damn, the man was beautiful. With his wool coat and glasses, he looked every bit the sexy librarian.

"Hey," Army said as he claimed the rocker next to Brit.

Brit tried tearing his gaze away without luck. "Hey. Your dinner is in the microwave."

Army kept his gaze locked on some point in the distance. "I'll put it in the fridge."

"Are you not hungry?" Brit didn't know how to be nonchalant when it came to Army.

"I've already eaten. I had a date."

Ouch. Army still wouldn't look at him, which turned out to be a good thing, since Brit couldn't hide his wince. "Oh."

At his response, Army finally looked his way. His gaze moved over Brit's face, as if searching for something only he understood. He leaned back in his seat and matched Brit's pose. Their shoes were inches from touching on the railing. "My co-worker, Linda, took me to dinner. Her sister is in town, and they don't get along. She needed a break."

"Oh." Brit didn't dare to say more. As it was, he didn't do a good job of hiding his relief. Thankfully, Army kept talking and saved him from a thousand confessions.

"On her fortieth birthday, her husband left her for some twenty-two-year-old girl who works at the coffee shop."

Brit sucked a breath between his teeth. "Ouch."

Army nodded but didn't look Brit's way. "I've been trying to convince her to rejoin the dating scene, but things are slim pickings around here." Army chuckled. The sound had chill bumps rising on Brit's skin. He'd felt that sound against his cock. Goddamn, he'd lost everything. "Sometimes, when we go out, I sit extra close to her, hoping people will talk and rumors will spread to her ex. Obviously, I'm not interested, but she's a gorgeous lady, and her ex is an idiot. He can't see that chick from the coffee shop only wants help with her tuition. Everyone knows she's sleeping with her foreign studies professor too."

Brit found himself sucked into the gossip. "I guess in a town this small, everyone knows everyone."

Army turned his head. Their gazes met. Brit forgot what they were talking about. "Don't worry. No one will call the press about you being here, or whatever it is you're worried about. My guess is that no one other than me has ever heard of *Vamps in Space*. This isn't the most imaginative place."

"No one knows I have any connection to this town, so I'm not worried, but that's not why I chose it," Brit admitted.

At his claim, Army dropped his feet and stood. "I guess I'd better put that food up and find you some blankets for the night."

Brit followed Army inside, silently cursing himself. He wanted everything fixed right this minute. It didn't seem that would be happening. He wasn't giving up. "What did you have for dinner?"

"Chinese," Army answered as he opened the microwave.

"You hate Chinese," Brit said without thought.

Army shot him a surprised look. "I can't believe you remember that. Since I wasn't paying, I can't complain," he said with a shrug. He pulled the plate from the microwave and stared down at it. "Did you make this?"

Even though Army wasn't looking at him, Brit shrugged. "I had time, and it's your favorite." He chuckled. "Although, I have to admit, I've never made roast before and it might have an English flair. Maybe you should be glad you ate elsewhere after all."

Army set the plate back inside the microwave and started the machine.

Brit hid a smile. "I ran by a small grocery store I passed on the way into town. They had a good meat selection."

"Wesley's."

Brit's eyebrows rose. "What?"

Army met his gaze. "Wesley's. That's the name of the store."

It was. Brit thought he should say as much and keep his end of the conversation going. Longing tightened his throat and forced a different confession from his lips. "I wish like hell I could take back everything I said, and you would stop looking at me like you hate me." Brit couldn't have stopped the words if he tried.

The microwave beeped. Army tore his gaze away and retrieved his plate. He turned his back on Brit as he found a fork. "I don't hate you," he said almost too quietly for Brit to hear. "How can I hate someone who cooked me a roast?" he added, flashing a smile over his shoulder. As Brit looked on, Army peeled off his jacket and tossed it on a nearby chair. Brit's feet stayed glued to the floor. His gaze didn't budge from Army. There was so much bitterness inside Brit for things he couldn't change.

Brit cleared his throat. "Still. I'm sorry."

Army set down the plate he'd just lifted and leaned against the counter. For longer than what could be considered comfortable, he stared at Brit in silence. "Come here."

Butterflies stirred in his stomach as he closed the distance between them, coming to stand toe to toe with Army. No matter how hard he tried, Brit couldn't uncross his arms.

Army's hand landed on Brit's crossed arms. He stroked once before his grip tightened on Brit's forearm. Brit tried breathing properly without luck. Army tugged, pulling Brit closer. Still, Brit refused to stop protecting his heart with his arms. Army dipped his head and touched his lips to Brit's in a quick kiss. Brit caught himself leaning forward, following Army's mouth like a magnet as the man pulled away.

"Thank you for dinner."

Brit stared at nothing as Army walked away with his plate in hand. They weren't fixed. Brit wasn't sure they would ever be what he wanted them to be again, but Brit had hope. He wasn't ready to walk away yet. Hopefully, Army wasn't either.

Chapter Three

THE WAY BRIT'S lanky body hung over the arm of the couch almost made Army feel guilty. Almost. After all, he hadn't forgotten Brit's claims of different men in every town. Each time he thought about Brit's parting shots at the conference, he wondered again why he'd agreed to let Brit stay here. He sure as hell didn't know why he'd kissed Brit.

Goddamn, Brit was adorable. Army couldn't stop watching him sleep.

Brit had fallen asleep wearing a hoodie with the hood on. His blond hair curled around the edge of the material. Army fought the urge to run his fingers through the man's hair, tucking the curls beneath. Brit had one arm slung over his eyes and his shirt rode up, exposing a delicious strip of flat stomach. Army sat on the coffee table, shoving spoonful after spoonful of cereal in his mouth just to keep his tongue busy. His lips tingled with the need to kiss that exposed skin. Army was beyond caring how blatant his staring had become.

With his bowl empty and nothing left to distract his hands, Army glanced around, desperately seeking anything else to focus upon. His gaze landed on Brit's bag. Were there drugs inside? A pain shot through Army's chest. He hated the idea of Brit transforming into that other guy again. After setting his bowl aside, Army stood and reached for the bag.

"There're no drugs in there," Brit said, sounding groggy and never uncovering his eyes.

Army wondered how long he'd been awake. "I didn't say there was. Can I put this away? I emptied a drawer for you."

"Sounds nice."

Without waiting for more, Army grabbed the bag and headed for his bedroom. He didn't know if the idea of searching Brit's things had him moving so fast, or if it was embarrassment over getting busted watching the man sleep. Either way, he still dug through the contents of the bag with zero shame.

There was a bottle of saline solution and a contact case on top. Army toyed with the items before setting them on the dresser. He hadn't known Brit wore contacts. The bag only had the essentials. Travel-sized toiletries and clothes. Army inspected every item inside the man's toiletry bag before setting it next to the contact supplies. While he folded each item of clothing, Army fought the urge to sniff each piece. The scent of Brit surrounded him, and Army couldn't stand the temptation. Brit reached past him and scooped up the items on the dresser before heading for the bathroom. Army watched his ass as he passed. His jeans sagged, needing to be pulled up, and making Army wonder if they were unbuttoned. The man was damn quiet when he walked. Army sent up a silent prayer he'd fought the urge to sniff Brit's clothing and hadn't gotten busted with the man's shirt pressed to his nose. He'd already gotten caught staring. For a moment, Army watched the closed bathroom door. He quickly brought Brit's shirt to his nose and inhaled. Damn, he loved the way Brit smelled. With Brit's things put away and nothing left to distract him, Army sat on the foot of the bed to wait. He stared at the bathroom door like the crazed fan he was. In fact, that was one of the many reasons Brit's parting shots had cut so deep. Army never forgot that Brit was Tanner Murray. As much as Army hated it, he was star struck by Brit. He still knew what it was like to be inside his celebrity crush. It didn't matter Brit was a real person —a person who'd stolen Army's heart. There was still a part of Army that knew he was also a fantasy come true.

The bathroom door opened and Army's mouth went dry. Brit still had his hood up. Those blond curls still needed to be tucked underneath. For a moment, Brit stood inside the open doorway with the light surrounding him like a halo. Army stared unabashed. Brit watched him as intensely. Without a word, Brit pushed away from the doorframe. Army watched as the distance between them disappeared. Then, Brit hovered over him. Army tilted his chin up to hold the man's stare. He didn't look away or say a word of protest as Brit straddled his lap and Army's back hit the mattress. Their lips met. Army made an important discovery. He wasn't angry or hurt any longer. They'd had a fight, and it was over. If Brit was an addict, it would come to light and Army would deal with it then. If Brit's claims had been more than that, and he'd actually gone to a different man in every town, that knowledge didn't change the fact that Army loved this man. Brit had swept him away in the past few months together. If he was being a fool, then it wouldn't be the first time. At least he could enjoy a moment of happiness before the pain.

ALTHOUGH BRIT HAD BEEN the one to initiate the kiss, he fell victim to it, as always. The instant their lips met, Army was in charge again. Their lips brushed, met, and lingered. Army's tongue swiped Brit's bottom lip. The moment he let Army inside, the man licked the roof of his mouth. He was a tease. Brit was captivated. Even though Brit was turned on, all of that was secondary to the emotions sitting on his chest. He knew why Army was the only person he'd slept with more than once. Maybe Brit lied to himself, and to Army, about more things than he could count, but Brit understood why Army was the only man he couldn't resist. Brit loved him.

Not that it mattered. He'd never confess his feelings, and he hoped Army didn't feel the same. Brit was here because he was selfish. He needed more time to create memories with Army. But that was all this time would amount to being. One day, be it tomorrow or six months from now, Army would hate him. He'd look back on this time with Brit and hate himself for wasting any energy on Brit. It was inevitable. For now, the sensation of Army's tongue against his and the man's flavor filling his mouth was everything to Brit. The way Army's body felt pinned beneath him and the beat of Army's heart against him kept Brit from moving on.

Army stroked Brit's jaw and tore his mouth away. "I have to get to work."

A loud groan grew in Brit's throat. "Are you joking?"

"Unfortunately, no," Army said while still trying to kiss Brit. "I was late getting back to work when you showed up here. I can't be late again this month or they'll write me up."

Brit rolled to the side, freeing Army. "I know how much you love your job."

Army didn't move right away. He turned his head and met Brit's stare. "It's not the only thing I care about. Maybe I can make it by on my lunch break."

Fuck. Brit recognized another lie he'd been telling himself. All the speeches Brit gave himself about not wanting Army's love were bullshit. "I'll be here whenever you can get home." Brit had never meant anything more.

Army bit his lip, visibly biting back a smile.

Brit couldn't take the sexiness. "I'll pay off every bill you have if you'll stay home with me."

"You drive a hard bargain," Army said with a laugh as he rolled to his feet. "But I can't leave Linda in a lurch." He stared down at Brit and turned serious. "And I could never live with you thinking I want a cent of your money."

Brit didn't know how to respond. He didn't want to insult Army. "Then I'll spoil you when you get home."

With one final sexy smile, Army left Brit alone, staring at the bedroom ceiling. He'd already paid off Army's car. No doubt, the man would be unhappy when he realized what Brit had done. Brit wasn't bothered by the thought. In fact, he wondered if he could do more—something Army wouldn't realize until after Brit was gone. A parting gift. He'd have to think on it. Army didn't want Brit's money. Brit didn't have anything else to offer, but lies.

THE ROOM WASN'T dark enough. Even when Brit closed his eyes, he could still see a hint of daylight. He didn't miss hotel beds, but he'd kill for their blackout curtains. The slight pressure behind his eyes kept him from covering them with his arm. He suspected the pressure would explode into crippling pain any moment. Sometimes, he could stop it from taking hold. He wasn't sure today would be one of those days. A door slamming nearby vibrated off his brain, making things worse.

"You paid off my car." Even though Army hadn't exactly yelled, his voice was still loud enough to turn Brit's stomach.

"So?" Brit kept his eyes squeezed shut, hoping to quell the nausea.

Army climbed onto the bed. "What do you mean, so? I told you I don't want your money."

To an extent, Brit had known Army wouldn't be happy when he realized Brit had paid off his debt. He hadn't expected Army to be this angry or to figure out things so quickly. "It's no big deal. When I heard you on the phone, it was obvious you were stressed. My boots cost more than what you owed. I can skip my next shoe purchase and be square." The silence following his claim had Brit peeking one eye open.

Army was staring at the open bedroom doorway. When he finally responded, he sounded horrified. "Are you talking about the work boots sitting by the front door?"

Brit shrugged. "Yeah."

"Jesus Christ," Army breathed. "That's... I don't even know what to say."

Brit shrugged again. He couldn't handle a spat right now. "Like I said, it's no big deal."

"It is," Army argued. "At the convention, you said I only want you because of who you are. That's not true and paying off my car gives that claim credence it doesn't deserve."

Brit had too many things to say. He couldn't deny he'd thought about why Army really wanted him too many times to count. This was important to them both. "If it isn't true, then paying off your car can't make it be so." Army's expression said he wanted to argue. Brit didn't have the strength today. He traced the curve of Army's cheek. "Don't take this the wrong way, but you don't strike me as a man who'd watch *Vamps in Space*."

Army didn't take the bait, but he let the subject of his car go. "You sleep a lot."

A soft chuckle escaped Brit. "I suffer from debilitating migraines. When I feel one brewing, I try to find a dark room where I can relax."

A line appeared between Army's eyebrows. "Is there a prescription you can take?"

Brit shrugged. "They've prescribed me several things over the years. Unfortunately, they either make me ill or put me out of my head. It's better this way."

Army's gaze moved over Brit's face. His concern showed in his stare. "I have some tricks. Would you let me try?"

Considering how bad the pain could get, Brit fought the urge to tell Army no. Brit didn't want to risk being forced to take his meds. Since the pressure wasn't too bad, he took a chance. "If it pleases you to do so."

Army's smile made the risk worthwhile. "Don't worry. I'm good at taking care of people." With that promise lingering between them, Army crawled from the bed and disappeared from sight. He reappeared before Brit had time to miss him. "Lift up."

At Army's demand, Brit lifted enough for Army to slip a heating pad beneath his shoulders. It wasn't warm yet. That didn't explain the heat spreading through his chest. Army made him feel too much.

"Take these ear plugs to block out any sound." He handed Brit a set of ear plugs. "Let me put this mask on you first," he added, urging Brit to lift his head. "It's a cooling mask, but it'll also block out any light. Just relax and let me take care of you."

"I trust you," Brit said, letting Army slip the mask over his eyes. He shoved the ear plugs in before Army responded. He didn't need Army to say anything. Army's every action said he cared. Maybe

Army had agreed to come to Brit's room that first time because he liked a character on a show. Brit didn't believe for a second he'd kept coming back for that reason. He definitely hadn't chosen to forgive Brit and take care of him through a headache because of a character. Brit more than trusted this man. He believed in him. If Army thought he could heal Brit, Brit didn't doubt him.

The darkness and silence mixed with the heat and ice. Brit didn't know what to focus on. He tried to concentrate on breathing. Warm lips touched his jaw. Brit startled at the unexpected touch. He'd lost himself in Army's care. Now his whole attention was locked on trying to guess Army's next move. Another kiss brushed his neck. Brit's breathing deepened. His cock stirred. Army shifted lower, kissing Brit's chest. Brit's entire being was focused on Army's every move. Cool air touched Brit's stomach a half second before Army's mouth warmed his skin. With the ear plugs in, Brit could hear his own ragged breaths in his ears. He gripped the sheet beneath him to keep from lifting his hips in a silent plea. Army's fingers curled around the edge of Brit's sweatpants. He dragged the material down, setting Brit's erection free. A cry left him when Army's hot mouth closed around Brit's erection. Every sensation heightened from his lack of sight and hearing. Brit's hips left the bed, chasing Army's mouth when he pulled away. He was back, swallowing Brit's cock before Brit could cry out. Brit had never been so close to orgasm so quickly. Army was perfection. He kept the exact suction on Brit's dick to bring Brit to the brink of insanity. Brit focused on the building pressure. He didn't want the encounter to end, but he couldn't stop reaching for release. Brit tensed. His lungs seized. The world stop turning for the beat of a heart. Light exploded behind Brit's closed lids, setting his body ablaze. Ecstasy stole the oxygen from the room. The soft stroking of Army's tongue didn't stop until Brit was limp and gasping.

Army kissed a path up Brit's body until his lips touched the spot beneath Brit's ear. One of the ear plugs disappeared. "Best lunch break ever," Army whispered. "I need to get back. Sleep." He replaced the ear plug and his weight disappeared.

Brit wanted to go after Army, lure him back to bed. His muscles were like jelly. By the time he caught his breath, each breath came deeper. Exhaustion weighed him down. Sleep claimed him without mercy.

"Tell me something new about Brit," Linda demanded as they logged in the new book arrivals.

It was fun having someone like Linda to talk to. He knew Brit was real, but Linda was convinced Army was creating a character for her to enjoy. He was free to tell her everything because she didn't believe it. "He has a migraine today."

She made a clucking sound with her tongue he assumed was meant to be sympathetic. "My great aunt used to suffer from horrible migraines. I remember she would turn into a raging harpy who said the most horrible things to everyone. She never meant any of it and didn't remember more than half of what she'd said when they passed. It's the pain, you see," she said, patting Army's arm. "It's so bad it messes with the mind."

Army froze. Brit didn't remember the things he'd said to Army at the convention. Army had assumed it was drugs, but it could've been something he took for his headaches. "Do you know if she took any prescriptions for her migraines?"

Linda chewed her bottom lip and stared at nothing as she seemed to think it over. "I'm not sure. That was a long time ago. But, nowadays, I know they prescribe some pretty hefty painkillers for people who suffer from debilitating migraines." Linda gave him a sharp nod. "It never occurred to me, but I guess it's possible Aunt Faye took something that had her so out of her head she didn't remember what she'd done. That makes sense. You don't think about those things when you're young. That's good information for your book, though. You should look that up." A huge grin spread across her face. "How do you intend to take care of Brit while he's suffering?"

To Army's horror, heat crawled up his neck and exploded through his cheeks.

A loud snort escaped Linda, forcing her to bury her face in the book she'd been labeling. Her shoulders shook in silent laughter, making Army laugh. Several people shot annoyed looks their way. He didn't care. They were usually the ones reminding people to keep it down. When he had his laughter under control, Army tried gathering real advice. "What do you think I should do? Massage? Cook him dinner? I'm not sure how to make his day better, besides letting him sleep."

"I don't know," Linda said with a shrug. "We used to leave my aunt alone until she was better." She glanced at the clock. "Did you know you were supposed to clock out five minutes ago?"

Army's gaze shifted to the time. "Wow. This day flew by. Usually, Fridays drag."

Linda flashed him a smile. "It's because we were chatting. Time always flies when we're together."

"That's true," Army said, logging into the computer system and clocking himself out. With that done, he pressed a quick kiss to Linda's cheek, making her blush. "Guess I'll have to figure my Brit problem out on my own. Be bad this weekend; you deserve it."

She swatted at his arm, sending him on his way. "Go on. I've got half an hour left. See you Monday."

"You too," he said, tossing a wave over his shoulder as he grabbed his coat and headed for the door.

Halfway home, Army decided to grab takeout. The last thing he wanted was to bang around in the kitchen and wake Brit. Once the scent of food filled his car, Army felt a little better—like he'd done something productive. He hated that Brit was in pain. His stomach twisted in knots. He hated even more that he'd stormed off from the convention, thinking Brit was an addict. Army didn't know how to come back from that. It seemed he had more baggage than he thought. Brit was the first guy to get under Army's skin since his mom's death. To his shame, Army had thought he'd been mostly relieved since his mom's passing. It wasn't until he'd stared into Brit's dilated eyes that all the horrible memories had washed over him, reminding Army that a woman he'd once loved more than life had been slowly stolen from him by drugs. He was more bitter than he'd thought.

The house was dark as Army came through the door. He checked on Brit after dumping the food in the kitchen. It looked as if Brit hadn't moved since Army left. Army found himself making sure the man was still breathing. Brit's chest expanded with each breath he took. Army shook off the panic that had gripped him for a second. He'd been the one who found his mom. Army never wanted to live through that again. He flipped the switch on the heating pad since the safety timer automatically shut it down after three hours. At some point, Brit had thrown off the mask. Army scooped it up and headed for the kitchen. He tiptoed around since he wasn't sure if

Brit still had in his ear plugs. At the kitchen counter, Army fell victim to his thoughts. He stared into space, trying to decide what to do. In truth, he wasn't hungry and he kind of wanted to eat with Brit. Maybe he'd just crawl into bed next to him. He could keep his distance and let Brit sleep.

Army startled as a solid body pressed against his from behind, trapping him against the counter. Brit's lips brushed his nape.

"Mhmm, damn. Did I sleep all day?"

A pant escaped Army. He'd never been turned on as quickly as he was with Brit's body melded against his. "Yeah, I just got home."

Another kiss warmed his neck. "Fuck. I'll probably never sleep tonight."

"That's okay." He tried turning in Brit's arms, but Brit held him still. "I'm off tomorrow, so we can stay up all night if you want."

Brit's hand found its way beneath Army's shirt. "I expected a library would be open on the weekends."

Army tried holding on to his quickly scattering thoughts. "Um. Yeah. We are. But Linda and I are full time, so they have college students who work the weekend shift."

"Good. I like having you to myself." Brit's hand slid lower, cupping Army's erection through his pants. Army tried again to turn. Brit leaned into him, stopping him. "Nope," Brit said against Army's nape. "You make me useless when you kiss me. For once, you'll hold still and let me be in charge."

Jesus. Army couldn't breathe. "Feel free to be in charge anytime you want."

Brit chuckled. The sound vibrated against the back of Army's neck. Goosebumps rose on his skin. He'd gone back to work after his lunch break horny as hell. Now Brit's teasing had him fucked up.

Still, he didn't want to hurt Brit. "How's the head?"

"I'm good," Brit said against Army's shoulder. He loosened the button on Army's pants and slid the zipper down. "Turns out, you're a miracle worker." His hand dove inside Army's underwear. He stroked Army's cock. "Damn, Army. I've changed my mind. I need to taste your tongue."

At Brit's claim, Army exploded into action. He spun in Brit's arms and slammed his mouth down on Brit's. Their tongues entwined, both trying to get closer to the other. Army walked Brit backward until he had the man trapped against the bar that separated the kitchen from the living room. He tore at Brit's clothes. The man's t-shirt and sweatpants made it way too easy to strip the man bare. Army wasn't an overly aggressive man. There was something about Brit that brought out a different side in him. He pulled the man's hair and bit at his lips. When it came to Brit, Army was ruthless. He never hesitated to demand what he wanted.

With his fingers buried in Brit's hair, Army tugged, forcing Brit to meet his stare. "I want you to fuck me." It wasn't something they'd done. In truth, before Brit, Army had been exclusively a bottom. Life had just worked out that way. The type of men he attracted preferred things that way. With Brit, they hadn't even discussed it. Army had just fallen on the man—like he needed to claim Brit as his. Now he wanted the same from Brit.

A slow smile spread across Brit's lips. "I've always known you were perfect for some reason."

"Does that mean you're not opposed?"

Brit linked fingers with Army and headed for the bedroom. "Luv, since you leave me useless, I'm sure you haven't realized it yet, but I'm as twisted as they come. There's probably not anything you'd suggest that I wouldn't try."

Army fought the urge to overtake Brit and push him to the floor. Damn, the man moved with such confidence in his nudity. He had every reason, but it was sexy as fuck. Army was in love with this amazing man. The words lived on his tongue. He fought to keep them to himself.

Once inside the bedroom, Brit tugged Army past him and urged him onto the bed. He set to work stripping Army. Since Army really wanted Brit inside him, he tried hard to be patient.

"I don't have any condoms or anything," Brit said, not meeting Army's gaze. For someone who claimed to be twisted and willing to try anything, Brit seemed unusually nervous.

Army leaned over the edge of the bed and found a box of condoms and some lube. He passed them

Brit's way. "I've got you covered." He paused for half a beat. "You don't have to do this."

Brit finally met his stare. The heat in Brit's gaze nearly scorched Army's skin. Army made an important discovery. It wasn't nervousness Brit tried hiding. It was intensity, as if he feared scaring Army away. Suddenly, Army was the one unbalanced. Brit's feelings were in his eyes, and Army wasn't sure he measured up. Because he needed something to do with his hands, Army ripped open one of the foil packets and rolled a condom down Brit's length. He coated the outside with lube. Damn, he wished Brit would make a move or say something. When there was nothing left to focus on, Army met Brit's gaze again. None of the fierceness had left Brit's eyes.

"I haven't slept with anyone else since I met you."

Army's mind went blank. He had nothing. Of all the confessions Brit could've made, that one hit the hardest. There was no way Brit could know how he'd struck the heart of Army's biggest fear—that he was only one of many. No one could see Brit's expression and call him a liar. He hadn't slept with anyone else since meeting Army.

Army licked his lips. He didn't want to ask. The answer might be more than he could handle. "Why?"

Brit's mouth slammed down on Army's with enough force their teeth bumped. Army let Brit urge him onto his back. His heart skipped a beat when Brit's chest touched his as the man covered Army's body with his. They fit in every way—like they were made for each other. The backs of Army's eyes stung. Brit kissed him like he loved him. By the time Brit draped Army's knee over his hip and pushed his way inside, Army's head was a mess. As many times as he'd told himself he was fine alone, Army would've expected to believe it by now. In that moment, he wanted to beg Brit to never leave. They felt more real than anything he'd ever had.

Brit took turns kissing Army and staring at him with heat in his eyes. Army was right there with Brit for every moment. With his weight braced on one elbow, Brit reached between them and jacked Army's cock in time with every pump of his hips. Army tried keeping up. He was useless. Nothing existed outside of Brit for Army. His body craved release. The pressure beating against his crown had him half insane. When his orgasm hit, Army lifted his head and claimed Brit's mouth to keep from screaming his love. Cum coated the space between them. Brit moaned against Army's lips. Army's heart squeezed in his chest. Between the high of release and knowing he was the reason Brit cried out in pleasure, Army floated on air. He worked twice as hard to make Brit come.

"I need to hear you scream," Army admitted as he fought to get closer to Brit.

Brit's thrusts quickened. His hips slammed against Army's ass. Army flattened his palms against the headboard to hold himself in place. Brit felt fucking amazing inside him. Every move the man made was sexy as fuck. Brit held Army's jaw, forcing Army to hold his stare as he came. Brit was a step beyond beautiful in his ecstasy. Army knew he'd never forget Brit's expression. It was hotter than any porn video Army had ever seen. He could jack off to the memory for the rest of his life. Army took a breath. His lungs burned, making him realize he'd been holding his breath while watching Brit own his pleasure.

Brit collapsed against him, uncaring of the mess between them. He grabbed a handful of comforter and covered their bodies as if Army's cum didn't coat their skin and a used condom wasn't ready to over-flow onto the bed. A random memory of something his mom had once said slammed into Army. *If a man doesn't care if he sleeps in the mess you've made together, that man loves you.* Army turned his head and eyed the beautiful man holding him. Tears pressed at the backs of Army's eyes. Life had never given him a damn thing but heartache. He prayed, just once, he could have this one thing for himself without getting hurt.

Chapter Four

EVEN THOUGH BRIT had only been with him a little over a week, Army craved these moments. The ones where they snuggled together, enjoying each other's touch. Turned sideways on the couch, Brit sat between Army's knees with his back against Army's chest. Army loved the way Brit felt in his arms. The man seemed to have an endless supply of super-soft hoodies to wear. He constantly stayed bundled up inside them. Army could close his eyes and feel the man's heat radiating through material against his chest and recall the man's scent, even when Brit wasn't around. His brain knew this arrangement was temporary. Army's heart refused to stamp on the brakes.

"You know what I've only now realized," Brit said, breaking the silence. "We're a week shy of Christmas and you don't have a tree."

For the hundredth time, Army found himself inhaling Brit's scent and tightening his hold on the man. "Why would I have a tree?"

Brit snorted. "Um, because it's Christmas time. That's what you do, isn't it? You decorate a tree and wrap presents. Sing carols and all that rubbish."

Army rested his chin on Brit's shoulder. "The only present I usually buy is for Linda. I haven't ever put up a tree."

Brit twisted in his hold, meeting his gaze. "Never?"

Army shrugged. There was no sense in reminding Brit he had no one to celebrate with.

"We should get one together," Brit said, brightening. "Surely this town has a tree lot."

"Do we have to get a real one?" Army asked, curling his nose. He wasn't very good at keeping plants alive. Much less an entire tree.

"Yes," Brit exclaimed as he jumped to his feet. "Don't worry. I'll take care of it. I'm aces at making green things flourish."

"Oh, you're serious. You want to go now?"

Brit nodded. "Of course. You've already almost waited too long. I bet all the good trees are gone. We'll probably have to get some shite little one, but my baby is getting a real Christmas this year."

A shot of horror raced through Army, even as he came to his feet. Brit had already paid off his car. "I say we set a spending limit."

"For a tree?" Brit asked, looking confused. "Baby, we can only fit so much in this living room. I don't think we have to worry about overspending."

"Not that," Army said, laughing as he stamped into his shoes. "I meant for presents."

Brit dragged a coat on over his hoodie and tugged on a stocking cap before pulling his hood up as well. "No. I promise I won't go overboard, but I won't swear to some tenner deal that'll just stress me out." Before Army had time to work up any irritation, Brit pulled him into his arms. "If I see something amazing and perfect that screams to be yours, I want to be free to buy it for you. If you want to ensure we stay even on this, then go with me to get a tree. Spend a real holiday with me—like it's our first in starting our own tradition. You're not the only one who's never had a normal Christmas."

Brit painted a picture Army couldn't resist. The man made it sound like this was only the first of many years to come. Even if it wasn't, Army wanted what Brit offered—a regular life. "Okay," Army said, relenting. "Let's go get a tree."

WHITE PUFFS FILLED the air with each breath Brit released. He fucking hated the cold. It was impossible to put on enough layers to stay warm. If he wasn't so driven to give Army the perfect Christmas, he never would've left his cozy spot on the couch in Army's arms. He smiled just thinking about it. They'd only been under the same roof for a little over a week, but Brit hadn't known there was so much happiness in the world.

"How about that one?" Army said, pointing toward a decent-looking tree and surprising Brit with his willingness to get into the spirit.

Brit eyed Army's choice. "I like it."

"Army."

They both turned at the sound of the female voice. A slender woman with zero curves but nice jet-black hair hopped in her excitement when she had their attention.

"I thought that was you."

"Linda, hey. Are you late getting your tree as well?"

This was Linda? Huh. Brit had expected her to look older.

She nodded. "Honestly, I almost didn't get one this year. It seemed a bit pointless. In the end, I decided I'd kick myself later if I let the holiday blues beat me." Her gaze slid Brit's way. She held her hand out. "Hi. I'm Linda. I work at the library with Army."

"Brit," Brit said, accepting her hand. Instead of shaking it, he drew her closer and brushed his lips across the top of her glove before releasing her.

"Charmed." Her nervous giggle made his ridiculous move worthwhile. Brit couldn't let Army's friend think he didn't have the best man possible.

She cleared her throat. "I'm sorry. Did you say your name is Brit?"

"A bit of humor on my father's part," Brit said. "He's British, but I was born during one of my parents' trips to America. He had to ensure I never forgot where I should've been born, but I'm ever the rebel." He clamped his teeth shut to keep from confessing more.

Army looked slightly confused. "I didn't know that."

Linda's gaze moved between them. She looked stunned.

The man working the lot walked by.

Brit didn't want to lose him, and he doubly needed to shut his mouth. "Apologies," he said, flashing Linda a quick smile before rushing after the fellow. "Excuse me. I'm interested in that one," he said, pointing out the tree they'd chosen. Brit was somewhat surprised Army didn't chase after him and browbeat him for paying. With his purchase made and arrangements set to have it carried to the car, Brit made his way back to Army. "We have our first tree together," he said, cutting into their discussion. "Now we just need to go buy some of those Christmas-shaped bits and bobs. What the bloody hell are they called?"

"Ornaments," Linda supplied.

He pointed at her. "Yes. Those. It was on the tip of my tongue, but I couldn't grasp it. I hate it when that happens."

"You're incredibly gorgeous," Linda said, surprising Brit so much he snapped his teeth together. "I have to admit, I thought Army had made you up."

"What an odd thing to say," Brit said, bemused.

She waved a dismissive hand. "Sorry. That didn't come out right. See, Army has been writing this book—"

"You ready to get out of this cold?" Army asked Brit, cutting Linda off and making her smile fall.

"Ah, he's using my hatred of the cold against me, but I'm determined to hear this story. Maybe I can come by the library sometime for a visit."

Linda brightened. "I'd like that."

"It's a date, then," Brit said, slinging his arm over Army's shoulders and starting away. "It was lovely meeting you," he called over his shoulder as he steered Army toward the car. "You're telling me about this book," he warned, making Army groan. For some reason he couldn't explain, the sound made his night.

ARMY REACHED past Brit to hang a porcelain gingerbread man on the tree. His fingers lingered on the ornament as his lips found the place where Brit's shirt met his neck. When Brit had suggested a tree, Army hadn't expected decorating it together to hit him in the chest. For the rest of his life, he would know this was his first normal Christmas, and he would remember who'd thrust it upon him. Army cast a wish to the universe he wouldn't look back on this night with sorrow. Brit hadn't moved in. They weren't partners. This was temporary. Any day now, Brit would leave. He'd return to a life Army couldn't compete with.

"Tell me about this book," Brit demanded, pulling Army from his thoughts.

"There isn't one." He wrapped his arms around Brit's waist and drew the man back against his chest. "When Linda's husband left, I started telling her stories to take her mind off things under the guise of working on a book. Rather than making her think I felt sorry for her, I made her believe she was helping me work through plot holes."

Brit massaged Army's forearms. "And that's what made her think I wasn't real?"

Army shrugged even as he kissed Brit's nape. "Maybe you're not."

He felt Brit tense. "What?"

"I don't know," Army said, struggling to explain. "Before you, I've never had a single wish come true." Brit relaxed in his arms. Army's lips moved from Brit's nape to the spot below his ear. "I dreamed and hoped for you—your kindness and your smiles." His hand moved to Brit's throat. He gently held the man in place as he nibbled on his ear. His cock hardened as Brit's ass moved against him—like Brit unconsciously sought him. "You're everything I've ever wanted and never expected to have. Maybe you're just a dream."

He felt Brit swallow against his light grip. Brit buried his hand between their bodies and rubbed Army's erection. The angle was awkward with Brit reaching behind him, but Army's dick didn't care. Brit's touch was all that mattered. It was everything he craved. "This tree will never get decorated at this rate."

A smile curved Army's lips that felt wicked even to him. "Did you know, I've already bought you one gift?"

Brit writhed in Army's hold as Army tongued the cords of his neck. "You must be feeling unusually cruel tonight, teasing me with your tongue and the idea of a present for me hiding somewhere in this house."

An evil-sounding chuckle vibrated from Army's throat. "I'm thinking I should let you have it a little early. Better yet, maybe I'll tell you what it is but make you wait."

"Jesus." Brit's harsh whisper only made Army more daring.

Army slowly dragged his hand down Brit's body, heading for the man's jeans. His palm itched to stroke Brit's sexy cock. "You said when I touch you, I make you useless," he said as he shaped the bulge in Brit's pants with his fingers. Brit sucked in a ragged-sounding breath. The sound drove Army to keep up the torture. "The way I figure it, you'll probably buy me some present I'll never be able to match, so I got creative. I'm giving you the gift of control. I bought you handcuffs. They come with a guarantee that you can use them on me any time you like."

Brit's chest expanded as the man sucked air. "They come with a guarantee, huh?"

Army lightly bit the shell of Brit's ear. "Yep."

"Then I'm calling it in now," Brit said, turning in Army's arms and meeting his stare. "I want you nude, on the bed, and restrained."

Army's dick jumped. No doubt the front of his underwear was soaked in pre-cum.

He wanted to capture Brit's lips. Instead, he walked away and headed for the bedroom. Army could feel Brit on his heels. Now that he wasn't holding Brit any longer, Army hoped he didn't chicken out. He'd never actually let anyone handcuff him before. The gift had been a spontaneous move. Telling Brit about the gift had been even more impetuous. Army pulled his shirt up and over his head while clearing his mind. He didn't want to think. Army wanted to feel. He reveled in the desire pumping through him as he shed his pants and underwear. Without thought, he stroked his cock. His eyes fell closed at the sensation of his palm teasing his over-sensitized nerve endings.

"Holy fuck. You're gorgeous."

Army's eyes shot open at Brit's claim. He'd almost forgotten he had an audience. Lust slowed his brain. He motioned toward the dresser. "The handcuffs are in the drawer under the clothes." As Brit dug through the clothes, Army climbed onto the bed. "Do you want me on my stomach or my back?"

"Your back," Brit answered while testing out the handcuffs and keys, as if he didn't want to make a mistake.

Army settled down in the center of the bed and obediently raised his arms above his head, waiting for Brit. "Whatever you want, I won't tell you no, but no tickling. I fucking hate that."

"Good to know," Brit said, flashing him an evil smile as he snapped one cuff in place before weaving the chain through a wooden rung and snapping the other one in place. Hunger radiated from Brit as he dragged his gaze down Army's nude body. As Army looked on, Brit stroked himself through his jeans before releasing the button. He slid his zipper down. Army's gaze never wavered. He held his breath, anticipating the first glimpse of the dick he craved. "You look so horny right now," Brit said, setting his cock free.

Saliva filled Army's mouth. He swallowed it down and licked his lips. "I swear I can taste you already."

At Army's claim, Brit's eyes flashed with desire. "I'm sure I can work something out," Brit said, stripping. "They say men think about sex quite often," Brit added once he was nude. He set one knee on the bed. "I can't remember how often, but when I'm with you, it's almost the only thing I think about."

"Almost?" Army squeaked out as Brit bent at the waist and lick Brit's erection from root to tip.

"I think about other things too," Brit confessed as he tossed one leg over Army's body, straddling him. He sucked Army's bottom lip between his teeth for a quick nip. "This mouth, for example," he said before inching higher on the bed. "I love tasting it and having it taste me."

Army almost sighed in relief as Brit finally made it high enough to offer Army the tip of his cock. "I think that falls under sex," he said before sucking Brit's crown. Their position made it impossible for Army to reach any other part of Brit's dick.

Brit's breath hitched hard enough for Army to hear. "Maybe," he said, bracing one hand against the headboard. "But those thoughts don't always feel sexual."

Army had no idea why Brit still sounded like he could formulate coherent thoughts. He tongued Brit's slit, trying to steal his reasoning.

Brit backed away, nearly causing Army to whimper. He slipped down Army's body, occasionally stopping to press a kiss to a new spot. When he reached Army's stomach, Army's cock strained to reach Brit's mouth. Brit had the most amazing tongue. Army craved its talent. Instead of giving Army what he yearned for, Brit shifted positions and rolled from the bed. Army wondered if he'd cry before this was over.

He was certain he would when Brit dug the box out from underneath Army's bed. Brit took his time pulling out condoms, lube, and—finally—an over-sized dildo.

Army's stomach cramped. "I think it's only fair to warn you, I've never actually used that. Linda gave it to me last year on Valentine's Day as a joke."

Brit fingered the huge fake cock. "I think, given the right incentive, you could take it."

Army wasn't as sure, but it looked like it was happening, nonetheless.

Brit climbed back onto the bed and popped open the bottle of lube. With his weight braced on his knees, Brit coated Army's balls. He urged Army's knees apart and took his time oiling Army's asshole. No matter how hard he tried, Army couldn't stop lifting his hips, openly fucking Brit's lubed fingers. A puddle of pre-cum soaked Army's stomach. He was leaking and moaning, straining toward pleasure he was nowhere near obtaining.

"Jesus, Brit." The harsh whisper was out of his control.

Brit's fingers disappeared.

A cry of denial escaped Army.

Brit coated the dildo while holding Army's gaze. "You look desperate for what only I can give you. I think this is quite possibly the best gift I've ever received."

Army automatically spread his knees wider as Brit rubbed Army's asshole with the lubed toy. He would've done anything—fucked whatever Brit offered—if the man would just set him free from the torment. Army gasped at the first intrusion. Brit went slow, retreating before pushing even deeper. Army's gaze sought for any purchase before landing on Brit's cock. It stood proud, tapping the spot above his navel. Pre-cum shined on the man's stomach. He wasn't unaffected. This torture went both ways. Army sucked in a deep breath. Another pulse of longing ran through him. Another drop of pre-cum dripped onto his stomach. Brit visibly sucked air as he fucked Army with the toy. Army had never been stretched wider. There was no missing all his hot spots with such a huge dildo. Army wrapped his fingers around the wooden rung and held on. He dug his heels into the mattress and openly fucked the fake dick in his ass. Brit shoved it deep and left it. Army fought to breathe. Brit rolled a condom down Army's length and was riding his cock before Army could think a clear thought.

On his knees with his head thrown back and Army's dick buried in his ass, Brit took his pleasure from Army even as he jacked off. Army couldn't even blink. His eyes itched from lack of moisture as he watched Brit. Army's senses were on overload. Every nerve ending was lit. The cries coming from Brit's throat were like music. The first jet of semen hit Army's chest. His body jerked involuntarily as a wave of ecstasy overtook him. He convulsed as Brit's tight ass milked every drop of cum from Army's balls. Still, he couldn't look away from the sexy man riding his cock. Their bodies were locked together, making them one person. He'd never felt closer to anyone. Army had never been more complete.

THE LIGHT SPILLING from the open bathroom door gave Brit all the incentive he needed to watch Army sleep. For the sixteenth time, he smoothed the blanket over Army. He didn't want to wake him. He needed to know his man was comfortable. There was also a bit of need to touch Army driving him. Brit had never felt like this. Not ever. Before Army, the only thing Brit had ever been passionate about was his work. Not only had Brit never dreamed his life could be like this, he never expected to want this.

Army rolled over, facing Brit, but didn't wake. Brit blatantly stared at the man who'd stolen him. His face was perfect. Army had been blessed with beautiful skin and sexy angles. Gorgeous lips. Brit's fingers itched to trace Army's jawline. Army had one of those unique jaws—that always seemed to flex. The man should've been a model instead of a librarian. Not that Brit was complaining. He loved the idea of no one knowing his sexy book nerd existed— like Brit had discovered a hidden treasure. Every day, Brit wished a little harder Army had found a treasure in him rather than a shit show, waiting to explode all over Army's life.

Brit lost the battle not to touch Army's face. He stroked the man's cheek. A smile curved Army's lips a half second before his eyes opened.

"Why aren't you sleeping?"

"I will in a minute." Brit hoped he wasn't lying.

Army's snaked his arm around Brit and dragged him closer, snuggling in tight. "Sleep now," he demanded, pulling a chuckle from Brit.

"It's hard with such a beautiful man beside me," Brit whined.

Army exploded into action, placing loud kisses all over Brit's face, making Brit's stomach hurt from laughing. Just as quickly as he'd exploded, Army settled back down with his face buried against Brit's neck. "You need a project. Sitting around all day has given you too much restless energy."

"Don't say that," Brit warned, running his fingers through Army's hair. "I might decide to start a class, teaching all the local housewives how to suck dick."

"You'd be amazing," Army said, sounding more asleep than awake.

Brit smiled into the darkness. "Or I might redecorate."

"Whatever makes you happy, baby." Army's words were slurred.

Brit's smile grew. It might be a blessing Army probably wouldn't remember giving, but Brit wouldn't let that hold him back. Brit fully intended to take over Army's life and give the man everything he didn't know he needed.

To LINDA'S CREDIT, she made it through the weekend without calling to get answers. She also managed to make it through three hours of working without bursting at the seams. By the time she finally broke, Army was ready to hand over the information without her asking.

"So," Linda said, sounding too much like she was going for disinterest. "Brit seems nice."

Army continued cataloguing resources. "He is."

"I hope I didn't offend him by saying I thought he wasn't real."

"You'll have to dig deep if you want to break through Brit's confidence and land an insult," Army said, still not looking her way.

"That's good. Of course, that doesn't change the fact I'm still mad at you."

Army's head whipped around. His gaze landed on Linda. "Me? What did I do?"

"You let me think he was a story you'd made up," Linda said, sounding upset.

Army turned on his stool and gave Linda his full attention. "I'm sorry." Army meant it. He would never hurt her. "It's just that I don't think we have any real future." It pained Army to admit such a thing, but it was the truth. "When Brit goes away, I figure it will hurt a little less if I can trick myself into thinking he was never real." He shrugged. "That probably sounds nuts. It's just that he's so far out of my league, and I don't know..." He trailed off, feeling defeated now that he'd admitted too much.

Linda slammed the three-ring binder she'd been holding down onto the counter. "Enough of that. Brit is the one who's lucky to have you. You're gorgeous and steady. Most of all, you're loyal, and that's worth its weight in gold. Brit had better be too, or I'll hunt him down and unman him."

A low chuckle escaped Army. "He's really amazing," Army admitted on a whisper, slightly embarrassed to admit how bad he had it for Brit.

"Who's really amazing? Am I being thrown over?"

Army heart raced into his throat at Brit's unexpected appearance. Heat climbed up the back of his neck over getting busted bragging. Army pasted on a fake smile. "Our boss," Army said, lying. "He's giving us a four-day weekend for the holiday. You're here," he tacked on before Linda called him out.

Without warning, Brit leaned over the counter and stole a kiss before backing away again. "I couldn't stay away. Would you like to go to lunch?"

"Um." Army checked the time on his computer. "Sure. Just let me clock out." He logged into his time sheet and made note of the time before closing out the screen. "Okay. I'm ready," he said, gathering his coat. He tossed a wave Linda's way. "I'll see you in an hour." After linking fingers with Brit, they headed for the door. Army waited until they were outside before peppering Brit with questions. "What have you been up to today? What made you decide to stop by? Ooh, what do you want to eat?" he tacked on, incapable of giving Brit time to answer.

Brit's laughter made Army smile. "I've been working on my new project. More specifically, your Christmas present. As I said, I couldn't stay away. I needed to see you. What are you in the mood for?"

Army turned and walked backward. Happiness filled his chest—like always when Brit was near. "You."

"Me?" Brit asked, sounding confused but still smiling.

"A kiss," Army explained.

Brit pulled the dark-blue stocking cap he wore under his coat's hood down before scratching his chin. "Hmmm, that seems a pretty sparse meal."

"Well, if you don't want it," Army said with an offended sniff before turning away.

A low growl sounded at Army's back, causing his breath to catch in his throat. Brit snagged the back of his neck, pulling him to a stop before spinning Army in his arms. "I want it."

Army's insides turned to mush at the lust in Brit's voice. Goddamn, he was in love. Brit made him strong and weak. He scared Army shitless and filled him with limitless courage. Brit licked Army's bottom lip. "But I can want it, and feed you. Let me spoil you."

It was hard to deny Brit anything with the man's tongue brushing his skin. "Only if you let me spoil you too."

Brit gently held Army's face between his hands. He brushed noses with Army while grinning like a fool. "You already do, baby. You already do."

It felt like the truth in Brit's arms. "I'd give you anything."

The wicked-looking smile pulling at Brit's lips had Army clinging to the lapels of the man's jacket. "Give me you," Brit demanded, going back to brushing noses with Army.

"You have me."

Brit pressed a light kiss to the corner of Army's mouth. "Yeah, but I want you to love me as much as I love you."

The rest of the world disappeared, along with all the oxygen. Not only had Army never dreamed Brit would love him, he doubly never expected the man to say the words. Even though his throat was like sandpaper, Army refused to let the moment pass unnoticed. "You already have that too."

While cupping Army's jaw between his hands, Brit's gaze moved over Army's face, as if searching for the truth behind his claim. "Say it."

Army didn't play dumb. "I love you."

Brit pressed his forehead to Army's while still holding his stare. "I love you too," Brit whispered, somehow doing what he always did best, making every moment between them beautiful.

Chapter Five

Valentine's Day...

Time moved in a blink of an eye. That's how damn happy Brit made him. All the ways Brit had taken over his life were apparent everywhere Army looked. From Army's redecorated office, complete with rotating bookshelves that held four times the books, that Brit had given him for Christmas, to the new kitchen table they sat at, showed how Brit spoiled him. Army wished he could give Brit even a quarter of what Brit gave him. The present burning a hole in his pocket also scratched at the back of Army's brain. He'd wiped his sweaty palms on his thighs too many times to count.

"I can't believe you did all this for me and managed

to do it without me knowing," Brit said, eyeing the flowers, champagne, food, and candlelight covering their new kitchen table.

"Linda helped," Army reminded him for the fifth time. If she hadn't agreed to coax Brit to the hairdresser with her to help her pick a new style for her date tonight, Army never would've pulled off the surprise dinner.

"This is delicious," Brit said, digging into the chocolate volcano cake Army had made for him.

"I like cooking, but you usually beat me to it," Army said, hoping he wouldn't be sick. He'd never been more nervous in his life. "Which is fine with me," Army added with a laugh.

Brit set his spoon aside and gave Army his full attention. "I have to be honest with you. After going a bit overboard for Christmas, I wasn't sure what to get you for Valentine's Day. I know you liked all your gifts, but I also know I made you uncomfortable." Brit's mouth lifted in one corner in the self-deprecating way Army couldn't resist. "I didn't want to make you feel that way today. So, my gift is super underwhelming, but it's from the heart."

Army's nervousness fled. "Having you sitting across from me right now is all the present I need."

"Still," Brit said with the world's sweetest smile. He pulled a folded piece of paper from his back pocket and slid it across the table. Their fingers brushed as Army reached for the paper. That one-time touch went straight to Army's heart. He unfolded the pages. It was a note. There were tiny hearts drawn in the margins. A smile pulled at the corners of Army's mouth at the corniness of the gift. It was a love note. Brit couldn't have given him anything better.

Army,

Sometimes it's hard for me to pull back. I want to buy you all the things. You have no idea how tempted I was to take you house shopping. Jesus, you make me a mess.

Army glanced up. "I'm so glad you didn't buy me a house. My pride would never recover."

Brit sipped his champagne. The candlelight shimmered off his gorgeous eyes. He looked so damn hot. Army tore his gaze away and focused on the note to keep from dragging Brit to the bedroom.

The day we met, I knew right away I'd met someone who would change me. There was a ripple in the air. A shift in my chest. Then we kissed. There hasn't been a thought in my head other than you since that first brush of lips. It took me a few months to realize it was love that consumed me. I'd never been in love before you. You'll have to forgive me when I'm too much. I don't know how to half arse anything. If I haven't told you lately, then Valentine's Day seems the perfect day to do so—I love you. You're amazing. There's no excuse for no one to have set the world at your feet before me, but I'm damned glad everyone you met before me was too stupid to give what you deserve. I can't imagine going a day without you in my life. There'll probably come a day when you realize I'm a complete piece of shit, and you'll rightfully toss me out on my ear. When that day comes, please keep this note somewhere you can revisit it, because I need you to know nothing is as permanent as the way I feel about you. That can't be faked. This thing between us is the realest reality that's ever existed. The world could strip everything else away from us, even our names, and the way we feel would still stand. So, refold this note, find a safe place for it, and let's go to bed.

—Brit

Army blinked several times. He'd never had anyone love him the way Brit did—not even his own mother had put him above all else. As he refolded the letter, Army came to his feet. He set the note on the kitchen counter, making a mental note to find a place for it tomorrow. Army's feet carried him to Brit's side. His plans for the night took a backseat to his raging emotions. Brit always left him too full.

He held his hand out to Brit. "Let's go to bed."

Brit blew out the candles before accepting Army's hand. Army could feel the man's heat at his back as they headed for the bedroom. Before he reached the door, Brit's lips brushed the back of his neck. Army sucked in a ragged breath, barely holding himself together. Brit would never understand how much it meant to have someone love him the way Brit did, and all the revelations in the universe didn't change the fact that one day Brit would have to return to his life. Even Brit's letter hinted at the lack of permanence between them.

He stripped Brit's clothes from his body, trying to focus on the present and what he could have now.

No amount of talking himself down or counting his blessing quelled the ache blooming in Army's chest. He loved a man destined to leave him. Once Brit was gone, Army feared what would be left behind— ghosts, a tattered soul, and nothing else. Sometimes, he wondered if the light Brit had brought into his life was worth the darkness he'd leave when he was gone.

Two hours into working, Army knew he wouldn't make it the entire day without seeing Brit. No doubt, Linda was probably getting tired of Army skipping out for lunch, especially since he rarely made it back on time. Thankfully, she didn't say a word as he clocked out and headed for the door. It took ten minutes for him to get home, and it would take ten more for him to get back. That left Army forty minutes to do as he pleased with Brit. What Army wanted was to leave the man panting. He didn't realize he was smiling until he felt the expression slip away. A black SUV sat in the driveway, and Brit's rental was missing. Since the front door stood open, Army assumed Brit was home. The only scenario that made sense was Brit changing rental cars again. He'd done so three times already, since he'd been in town much longer than they'd antici-pated. A spark of hope lit Army from the inside out. Maybe Brit had finally bought a car and planned to stay for good. Army knew it was a longshot, but lying to himself about getting to keep Brit was how Army made it through most days. He parked his car on the other side of the SUV and headed inside.

The screen door slammed behind Army as he came cleared the doorway. "Hey, babe. What happened to your car and why is there a huge SUV out fron—" Army froze at the sight of a blond stranger in his living room.

The man turned at Army's appearance. "Hey, sexy. That's my security detail. They're here to pick me up." He held up a slip of paper. "Twenty-five thou-sand, as promised." He set the check on the bar.

Army stared hard at the carbon copy of Brit standing in his living room. They were exact clones, except this man was maybe an inch or two taller and his hair was lighter. "Who the fuck are you?"

The man blinked, as if confused by Army's question. "Tanner."

His voice was too deep. Army shook his head. "You don't sleep next to someone every night and wake up beside them every day without recognizing them. So, I ask again. Who the fuck are you?"

The blond rolled his eyes and repeated his earlier answer. "Tanner."

Realization dawned on Army—like he'd been living in a cave and stepped into the light. This was Tanner—the actor, the star... the drugged-out ninja. "So who's been living with me?"

One corner of Tanner's mouth lifted in a smirk. Army had never wanted to put his hands on someone in anger like he did this man who mocked his confusion. "My cousin, and doppelganger, Brit. Really, we do look amazingly alike, do we not? Of course, some of that is due to colored contacts and other artificial means, but still."

Army couldn't respond. They didn't look as much alike as they should, considering they'd fooled him at the convention. The door flew open behind Army, startling him, and saving him from finding words other than all the cursing rising in his throat.

"What the fuck are you doing here—" Brit froze. His gaze moved from Tanner to Army and back again before finally landing on Army. "Army, hey. You're home early. I didn't see your car in the driveway."

Without acknowledging Brit's greeting, Army moved to the couch and sat. His legs didn't want to hold him any longer. "I parked next to Tanner's SUV," he said, barely hearing the words, even though he was almost certain he'd said them. His gaze moved between them. Side by side, they looked more alike than Army wanted to admit. Tanner was taller—more polished. His hair was lighter and styled to perfection. Even the man's teeth gleamed like a million bucks. Brit was younger. While standing next to each other, the age difference was more than apparent. But people only saw Tanner on TV, where he was caked in makeup and looked younger than in reality, playing a vampire trapped forever in an eighteen-year-old body. Army fought the urge to put his head between his knees and suck air. He'd never questioned Brit's age, because he'd believed he was Tanner. Tanner's age was a computer click away. He was twenty-six—like Army. The man had been born in Lanchester Village in England. Everything about Tanner was a click away, except the fact that his cousin obviously spent his days pretending to be the famous actor. Fuck.

"How old are you?" Fuck all. He had no idea why that was the first question to breach his lips, but he had to start somewhere.

To Brit's credit, he held Army's stare without looking away. Too bad the man hadn't been braver before now—when it mattered. Before the lies piled up. "Nineteen."

Army's eyes fell closed. Goddamn. The guy wasn't even old enough to drink.

"I'll wait in the car," Tanner said, obviously intent on leaving with Brit.

Army had words for him too, but not as many as he had for the betrayer standing across from him. Silence filled the house until Tanner left them alone. The ticking of the clock was the only sound cutting through the tomb-like quiet.

Brit broke first. "Say something."

To Army's horror, his throat swelled. He swallowed past the pain. "You'd better get your things. Tanner is obviously waiting to take you away. Job fulfilled, or whatever I was."

"Army, I—"

"Grab Tanner's check on your way out," Army said, cutting him off. He couldn't listen to any more lies. "You already paid off my car." The pain was real and choking.

Brit crossed the room and came to stand over Army, forcing Army to tilt his head back to hold the man's stare. "I'm not leaving until you talk to me."

Army shook his head, fighting the tears that wanted to consume him. "There's nothing to say. You asked for a place to stay. I'm guessing whatever the real reason was for you hiding out is over."

Brit squatted between Army's knees. "Goddamn it, Army. There's a lot to say. Yell at me. Anything."

"I don't even know you." Army choked on the words. Everything he'd thought was real was a lie. "Why would I yell at a stranger?"

"I'll send you a resume," Brit said. He squeezed and rubbed Army's thighs, as if trying to soothe him.

"Why? Do you impersonate librarians too?"

Brit's chest expanded as he sucked in a deep breath. "It was a joke. I do that when I'm nervous."

"It seems everything is a joke to you, including me," Army said, uncaring how spiteful the blow had been.

"Fuck, Army. You know that's not true."

"The thing is, I don't," Army said, finding his words. "When I walked away from you..." He took a breath, and started over. "When I walked away from Tanner, I never thought I'd give you another shot. I never wanted another addict—like my mother—in my life. But then, you showed up at my door and proved you were different. I thought maybe I'd been wrong. Made a mistake. I thought you'd had an off day, and... fuck you," Army said, sounding tired to even his ears. "If you knew me at all, then you'd know whatever this is you're doing, I probably would've accepted it, if you'd just been honest with me."

Brit's lips were pressed together in a tight line. He gave Army a sharp nod. "I have a non-disclosure contract with Tanner," he said, as if coming to a decision. "Even if I didn't, I'm still not sure I would've told you." Brit pushed to his feet. He stared down at Army. "I loved the way you looked at me the first time we met, but you thought you were meeting him. Just like everyone else." A sad smile touched his lips before disappearing again. "If you'd met Brit Murray instead, I don't believe for a second you would've looked at me the same. I should go," he said, heading for the bedroom.

Army watched him go. He wanted to chase the man down—force him to explain. Instead, he stayed put. Army's gaze followed Brit's every move as he gathered his things. When Brit had everything in hand and stood at the door, he glanced Army's way one final time. The air seemed to hold its breath as they stared at each other.

"I'll send someone to pick up my rental. Cash that check," Brit said, delivering a final blow. "You earned it." Without another word, he left Army staring after him, bleeding on the inside.

REGGIE, Tanner's largest security guy, jumped from the car at Brit's approach. He relieved Brit of his bags. Brit slipped inside the vehicle before he changed his mind. A huge part of him still wanted to rush back inside the house. He needed to beg Army to understand and forgive him. Army's expression had said it all. He'd never forgive Brit. Too many lies stood between them. Brit wished there was a way he could make Army understand. Things between them had grown right alongside his lies. There'd never been any malice in Brit's heart. He hadn't set out to hurt Army. Brit had fallen in love with Army so easily. He'd forgotten all his deals with Tanner just as easily. It was like they'd been inside their own tiny world. Everything he'd been and done before Army no longer existed. Now, it did again. His two realities had collided with the appearance of Tanner. Brit had no one to blame but himself.

"Judging by your friend's reaction, he wasn't thrilled to learn you aren't me." Tanner wasn't a mean-spirited person, but he didn't think before he spoke. This was no different.

"That was our deal," Brit reminded him, barely hanging on to his shit. "No one knows I'm not you."

Tanner didn't respond right away. Brit met his cousin's gaze. The way Tanner eyed him, as if searching for some tidbit of information, set Brit's teeth on edge. He kept his cousin's reputation intact. Brit didn't owe the man anything else. If Tanner wasn't such a fuck-up, Brit might feel differently, but Tanner didn't make it easy to keep his name clean.

"I've never seen you with a man before this one."

Brit ground his back teeth. "What of it? It's not like you've spent a lot of time with me in the past few years."

Tanner shook his head. "I know we have a deal, but I'd never expect you to lie to someone you love and know you can trust. This was never meant to be a permanent arrangement."

Despite his best efforts, Brit's temper snapped. "No shit, Tanner. It was supposed to be *very* temporary. You were supposed to get your shit together. I didn't agree to this for the money, and I sure as fuck didn't agree to do this for the rest of my bloody life. You were supposed to get clean. I never wanted—" Brit bit off his words before he gave away more of himself than he already had for Tanner's issues. No one understood what it was like. He loved Tanner. They were cousins, but closer than brothers. Growing up, Tanner had been his best friend. Now he was an addict and nothing else. The shit the man put in his body had stolen the person he'd been, replacing him with an addict no one could love. No one understood, but Army. Brit's eyes fell closed at the thought. Army had already survived life with an addict. Then Brit had shown up and dragged another one into his life.

"Jesus, you really do love this guy. I never expected, I mean, you've always been..."

Brit met his gaze. "Straight," he supplied.

Tanner nodded. "Yeah, when I told you'd have to invite a few guys back to your room occasionally, since it's what I would do, I never thought this would happen."

Brit blew out a breath. "Honestly, I never thought it would happen either. I mean, I've always known I'm on the sexuality spectrum, but I've always been sort of apathetic about sex itself." He scrubbed his hands through his hair. Heat rushed to his cheeks. "Fuck." He couldn't believe the confessions racing to his lips. He thought the world of his cousin, but he wasn't one to talk about his personal life.

A bright smile stretched Tanner's lips. "You just hadn't met the right person."

"Obviously," Brit grumbled. The memory of the day he'd met Army slammed into him. Butterflies stirred in his stomach just as they did that day. All embarrassment fled. "He's the one and I just fucked up any chance of ever being with him again."

"Never underestimate my ability to weasel my way into someone's good graces," Tanner said with a laugh. "I'll fix this."

Brit nodded, even though he didn't put much faith in Tanner. After all, the man he'd grown up with had disappeared inside a pill bottle long ago, leaving Brit alone. He changed the topic. "How was rehab?"

Tanner shrugged. "It was rehab. Don't worry. It'll stick this time."

Army's words came back to haunt him. *That's exactly what my mom said every time right before I ended up in a new foster home.* "Yeah, of course. You got this," Brit agreed, even though he knew better. Army might have been horrified over Brit's true age, but Brit felt he had no reason to be. Tanner made him an old man a long time ago. Loyalty was a hell of thing. Sometimes, Brit wondered if he'd ever stop bashing himself against the rocks in hopes of saving Tanner. He was tired of being Tanner's face at conventions, because the man was too far gone to handle things himself. Brit was fucking exhausted with smiling and losing—like the way he'd lost Army. "Maybe this is a good time for you to reclaim your place at conventions. You've been gone a few months. It would be easy for you to slip back into the role without anyone noticing."

Tanner looked away and focused on something outside the window. "Maybe."

Brit's throat tightened. He'd never be free. Not unless he dropped his cousin, leaving him to his problems. That was one thing Brit didn't know if he could ever do. After all, blood was blood, and Brit didn't have anyone else. Not really.

ARMY HAD no idea how long he sat in silence, staring at nothing once Brit was gone. He was wiped clean. There was no other way to describe the devastation Brit had wreaked on his life. He'd like to think hindsight was twenty-twenty, but Army had been damnably clear minded in his dealings with Brit. Brit had shown up, offering him money for a place to stay. Army had thought every day he should make Brit explain why he needed a place to hide. He hadn't. It had been an intentional move on his part. Army hadn't wanted to learn a single damn thing about Brit that might risk the man leaving a single second sooner than necessary. Ignorance was bliss, and he'd been ecstatic in the dark.

Army's legs ached as he came to his feet—like losing Brit was the world's worst case of the flu. His gaze moved over the room. His home didn't look like his any longer. It was theirs. Over the course of four months, Brit had replaced damn near every stick of furniture. He shouldn't have let that go on. He focused on the flat screen hanging on the wall. A snort escaped him. Since Brit came to stay, he hadn't watched a single episode of *Vamps in Space*—not a new airing or a rerun. Maybe he'd been content to have the real man in his bed, as Tanner claimed. Or, perhaps—subconsciously—he'd known Brit wasn't Tanner.

He moved to the kitchen with no real plan. His feet ushered an empty shell. There nothing left of Army. Army froze, holding the handle of the fridge, unsure of why he even stood there. His gaze landed on a row of tiny red hearts drawn in the margin of a letter held by a magnet on the freezer door. He couldn't breathe. His eyes burned with unshed tears. He'd been conned. Brit had stolen his heart with pretty words and lies. Even the man's Valentine's Day letter looked different in the light of Brit's deception. How could one person be so cruel? Some of the numbness lifted, replaced by rage. He'd opened his home to Brit—loved him. A burst of anger-fueled insanity overcame Army. In one swipe, he cleared the kitchen counter, taking out several dishes and the microwave. It hung from the edge of the counter by the cord still plugged into the wall. Army's chest heaved as he stared at the mess. It wasn't enough to squelch the rage—nowhere near enough. He wanted to set fire to the house and watch it burn. Army hated every inch of the space he shared with Brit. Most of all, he hated himself for trusting Brit not to break him like this. Now there was nothing left for him, and there never would be. His mom had been right all along. He was a mistake no one would ever love.

Chapter Six

BRIT: *I'm in Canton. If you can make it, I've left you a gold pass at will call.*

———

555-6798: *This is Tanner. Would you please come see Brit in Canton? All of this is my fault. Please don't let all my shortcomings ruin what the two of you have.*

———

BRIT: *Canton might've been too far. I'm in Atlanta this weekend. I left a gold pass at will call.*

———

BRIT: *Okay. So, you're ignoring me still. Here's a list of all Tanner's upcoming appearances. I'll always leave you a pass. All you have to do is show up. Please?*

———

TANNER: *Seriously, our next show is literally a two-hour drive from you. I'm sick of watching Brit mope. He never would've lied to you if I hadn't made him lie to everyone. I'm the piece of shit. He's every bit as amazing as I'm sure he showed himself to be. Don't lose this because of me, please? I know you don't want anything to do with me, but it's not easy being the person who fucks up everything either.*

———

"ARMY."

Army turned at the sound of his name. "Jaylah. Wow. What a small world."

She shrugged. "Maybe not so much in the convention world."

"That's true," he agreed. Discomfort replaced his burst of happiness over seeing a familiar face.

Jaylah didn't seem to suffer the same. "Are you here stalking Tanner? I am," she added, not giving Army time to answer. She snagged his arm and dragged him along. "Come on. His line is over here."

Army tripped over his feet trying to keep up. For a short girl in stacked boots, she could move when properly motivated.

Once they had their spot in line, she turned on him. "You never tracked me down to let me know what happened with Tanner at the last convention. Spill."

Army shrugged. His discomfort doubled. "Nothing happened. Someone who works for him met me to retrieve the jacket. We never spoke." It wasn't a total lie. Tanner hadn't shown up until much later.

Jaylah visibly deflated. "Dude, that sucks."

"It's not a big deal," Army said, waving off her words. "I tried hunting you down afterward, but I couldn't find you in the crowd, and I had to work the next day." Lies rolled easily from Army's tongue. He hadn't known he had it in him. Maybe he should be acting too, or Brit had rubbed off on him.

"Obviously, him not showing up hasn't ruined your love of the show."

A smile that felt fake, even to Army, stretched his lips. "Of course not. To be honest, I didn't expect him to show."

Jaylah made a noise that could've meant anything at all. She eyed the line, going up on her toes. "How long do you think we'll have to wait this time?"

Army hoped they never made it. He didn't know what to say or do. In fact, he didn't know why he'd shown. That wasn't true. He needed answers, and he had things to say. All those unspoken words were trapped inside his head, making him insane. Army counted the people ahead of them. "Maybe twenty minutes," he guessed. Unlike last time, he didn't continually glance Brit's way. He couldn't. If they made eye contact, he might lose his nerve and run.

"I went to the show in Canton," Jaylah said, keeping Army from bolting. "The lines there were awful. Probably because Tanner has been in rehab and it was his first show back. Anyhow, I had to wait like two hours to get an autograph, and you'll never guess who I ran into."

Army's brain hiccupped. "Rehab? When was this?"

Jaylah stared at him as if they'd never met. "Do you live under a rock? It's been on all the gossip talk shows and some of the major networks as well."

"I've been busy at work, and..." Army couldn't think of a good lie. "Anyway, Tell me."

Jaylah perked up, obviously delighted to be the first to tell someone who hadn't heard, and dropped her goth act. "It was right after the show where we met. He was supposed to announce his new role in some ninja or samurai movie. Whatever. Anyhow, supposedly, he flipped out in his room and did like thousands in damage, smashing furniture and shit." She paused and stared at him as if seeing nothing. "Come to think of it," Jaylah said suddenly. "Maybe it's a good thing he didn't show to meet you. Can you imagine?"

"No," Army lied through numb lips. "What happened after he trashed the room?"

Jaylah shrugged. "He paid off the hotel and agreed to go into rehab."

The line moved, and Army shuffled forward along with it while staring at nothing. So, the real Tanner was an addict. If Brit had been covering for him, it would make sense he'd need a place to stay out of sight until Tanner finished rehab. Army puffed out his cheeks and blew out a breath. He didn't know what to do or think. As much as he wanted to be angry with Brit, Army understood covering an addict's ass. He couldn't count the number of times he'd lied and done things he'd never thought himself capable of to hide his mom's problem.

"Oh," Jaylah said, smacking his arm. "I forgot to tell you who I saw in Canton. Jay."

Army tried hard to seem interested. "The herpie-ridden ex?"

"The one and only. You'll never guess who he was with."

"The herpie-ridden ex best friend," Army guessed.

"Yep," Jaylah said, scowling. "Conventions were our thing. Boyfriend-stealing bitch."

Despite everything, Army caught himself smiling. "I'd tell you to go after her ex, the mage or whatever, but we've already decided he's probably the founder of the STD issue."

Jaylah hugged her autograph book to her chest. "I hate men. Not you, of course," she clarified. "You're gay, so you don't count."

Army hummed, unsure of how to take that. "Are giving up on the hetero life, then?" Army had to keep some form of conversation going. He was about two seconds away from shaking to the point he was seasick. Even though Brit had left him a ticket, that didn't mean they were okay. Jesus, he was a mess.

"I'm not sure," Jaylah answered, sounding thoughtful.

"Maybe you should wait a little longer before switching teams," Army offered. "That guy over there hasn't stopped staring at you since we got in line."

Jaylah glanced in the direction Army motioned. "Damn. He's got that needs-someone-to-save-him vibe I love. My luck he's looking at you, though."

Army glanced the guy's way. He was tall and wiry. The guy didn't look like he matched with Jaylah at all, but someone should be happy. Army didn't know if he ever would be again. "Nope. He's straight."

"How do you—" The line moved, cutting off Jaylah's question. "Oh my god. We're next. I'm definitely asking for a hug this time."

"You should," Army said, staying loyal despite the sudden urge to puke. No matter how hard he tried, Army couldn't stop staring at his shoes. They'd cost him around fifty dollars on sale. Brit paid more than ten thousand for a pair of boots. What in the hell was Army doing here? They didn't match. Suddenly, he was at the edge of the table, and there was nowhere to run.

"Damn. You're hot."

Army's head jerked up at the words. Blue eyes waited for him. It was Tanner. The real Tanner. Army's brain couldn't reconcile what his eyes showed him when he'd been waiting to see Brit. "It's crowded," Army said, idiocy setting in. "Too much body heat."

Tanner chuckled. It was sexy. Army wasn't immune. "I meant you, Army. You're incredibly sexy."

"Jaylah wants a hug," Army said, pushing her forward and selling out his friend without shame.

Tanner's gaze shifted Jaylah's way. He became the movie star. "Is that so?" Tanner came to his feet. "Hand your phone to Army, and he'll take our picture."

Jaylah shoved her phone Army's way.

Tanner's personal assistant and handler, a woman with tired brown eyes and an unfriendly demeanor, tried interceding. "Tanner, everyone will want pictures with you if you start. You need to get through the rest of this line before the next panel."

Tanner waved off her concerns. "I won't do any more after this one. Army is a friend." He winked.

A hint of bitterness wormed its way into Army's heart. Tanner was all charm. His bullshit had broken Army's heart. Maybe it had been Brit's lies, but he'd lied because of Tanner's bullshit. Army snapped three pictures, uncaring of how they turned out.

He'd shown up for Brit. Damn, he was tired of wasting his time.

Tanner hugged Jaylah one last time before sending her away squealing, all pretense of goth-hood gone. The lanky redhead stole his chance to meet her, gushing over the pictures Army had taken. Tanner shrugged off his leather coat and held it out to Army. When Army didn't reach for it, Tanner leaned in and spoke close to Army's ear. "Take it. There's a room key in the inside pocket. You showed up. Go see him."

Army accepted the coat.

Tanner didn't release it right away. Their gazes met. "I'm sorry."

Army's throat swelled. Tanner meant it, but Army wasn't sure the man's apology changed a damn thing. He dipped his chin and Tanner released the jacket.

Tanner took a step back. "It was good seeing you again, Army." He reclaimed his seat and went back to charming the crowd.

Army tried hard not to look at anyone. He ducked his head and headed for the door, hoping he could get away before Jaylah spotted him. As he power-walked toward the lobby, Army dug through the inside pocket until he found the key card. It was still inside the envelope the hotel handed out with the room number handwritten on the outside. 335. Army turned the card over in his hand. He could turn around and march back to Tanner, giving up the jacket and key. There was no law that said he had to see Brit ever again. One thought stopped him from walking away—Tanner had given him his coat. Just as Brit had done the day they'd met. The only way Tanner could've known that was if Brit had told him the story—like Army was special. He to know. Before he could change his mind, Army headed for the elevator. It was too late to walk away now. He had to know.

HOTEL AFTER HOTEL, they all felt the same—like he'd never have a home again. He should've gone home when Tanner agreed to return to playing at his own life, but Brit couldn't leave without seeing Army first. There were three more stops on this year's convention tour. If Army didn't show, Brit would have to face the truth. They were over. Army would never forgive him. Too many times to count, he'd taken out his phone and thought to call Army. Force him to talk. Beg for forgiveness. The thing was, he really needed to do that face to face, and he wouldn't force his presence on the man again.

Today, he was twice as restless than usual. Stress wasn't good for him. He hoped he didn't end up bedridden with a migraine before the end of the day. He tried concentrating on his breathing and doing all the things he'd been taught to avoid triggering a headache. Brit couldn't focus. He wanted to tear off his skin.

"Do I need to hunt down a set of ear plugs and an eye mask?"

Brit spun at the unexpected question. Army stood, holding Tanner's jacket and looking unsure of his welcome. The desire to tackle the man to the floor and refuse to let him leave nearly crippled Brit. He ate up the vision of Army. Even his eyes missed the man. He tried tempering his voice.

"I've taken to traveling with those items, just in case."

Concern etched Army's features. He set Tanner's coat on the chair beside the door. "Are you in pain?"

Brit swallowed past the lump in his throat. "Yes." His answer came out in a scratchy whisper. He'd never hurt more in his life, but it had nothing to do with his head.

Army's gaze moved over Brit's face. "What do you need me to do?"

"Tell me I'm not the only one gutted," Brit said before he could stop himself. "Tell me I haven't lost every chance of having you love me, because I let Tanner completely muck up my life." Brit took a step toward Army.

Army didn't back away, but his expression gave nothing away. "Do you want me to still love you?"

"I'm not sure it matters," Brit answered honestly. "It won't change the fact that I love you enough for both of us."

Army's eyes fell closed for a moment, as if Brit's words physically hurt. When his eyes reopened, he looked crushed. "You're a complete stranger to me."

Brit felt the blow of Army's claim like a sledgehammer. He didn't understand how he could be so intimate with Army, and Army feel like they'd never met. He couldn't find the words to respond. Army had stolen his voice.

Army moved Tanner's jacket to the arm of the chair and sat. He focused on Brit. "I never asked any questions about your life because I thought I knew. How can you love someone who never bothered to learn anything about you?"

Brit moved to the couch across from him and sat. Army didn't sound like a man who no longer cared. As long as Army stayed and kept talking, there was hope. "I would've been forced to lie, so I'm glad you didn't ask."

"What about now?" Army shot back.

"Ask anything you want. I promise to be honest."

Army cast a quick glance around the room, as if searching for a place to start, before meeting Brit's gaze again. "When is your birthday? What's your favorite color? Do you even like *Vamps in Space*?"

"February second. My favorite color changes with my mood. I think people are more critical of things when they know someone involved personally. Like, if your friend writes a book, or your cousin plays a vampire on TV. I have a hard time connecting with *Vamps in Space* because all I see is the boy I grew up with, pretending to be someone else."

Army's expression turned pained. "You were staying with me on your birthday, and I didn't even know it. Do you know how much it breaks me, knowing your birthday was stolen from you, because you were playing at being someone else?"

Brit shook his head, fighting back his emotions. "It wasn't stolen from me. You made every day special, but on February second, you took off work and stayed home with me. We cuddled on the couch and watched that web series you'd read about. Afterward, you set your laptop aside and kissed me. For the longest time, you held me and switched between kissing me and talking about nothing at all. It was the best day I'd had in as long as I can remember. If you'd known it was my birthday, I still wouldn't have wanted anything different."

Army sat forward and set his elbows on his knees. His blue t-shirt made his eyes stand out even more than usual. His glasses couldn't hide their beauty. "I don't understand the paying off my car and ten-thousand-dollar boots. Is that just part of playing Tanner?"

A small smile tugged at Brit's lips. "Just because I'm not really Tanner Murray doesn't mean I'm no one. I've never spent a dime of Tanner's money."

Army's expression still didn't change. "What about the rest of the people from the show? They had to know you're not Tanner."

"Of course they did. They've done a lot of covering for me on the panels when I didn't know how to answer fan questions."

A deep line appeared between Army's brows. "Why would they go along with this?"

Brit's eyebrows hit his hairline. "You spent ten minutes in Tanner's company at the last convention, and you never wanted to see him again. Trust me, everyone around here was damn relieved Tanner wouldn't be part of the tour. At least as long as he was using, anyhow."

Army shook his head. "I just don't see how you've gotten away with this."

"Money," Brit said, taking it to the bare bones. "The show is on its last season and the cast makes a ton of money on these conventions. Tanner is a huge draw. Not to mention, body doubles are a common thing in this business. Actors can't be everywhere at one time."

"You know I'm in love with you. How could you wake up next to me every day and lie like I meant nothing?"

Army's question came from left field and sucker punched the air from Brit's lungs.

Unfortunately, Army wasn't finished. "How could you kiss me with someone else's lips? How could you make love to me when you knew you'd have to come clean or leave?" Army's eyes filled with tears. The shards left of Brit's broken heart shattered at the sight. He hated knowing it was his fault. "Don't bother answering," Army said, shoving the final knife in Brit's chest. "Because I don't know how to believe anything you say."

Army stood.

Brit flew to his feet. "Please, don't leave."

Army was the picture of devastation. His eyes were bloodshot and the tip of his nose was red. He visibly struggled for air. "Why?"

Brit couldn't take the space between them any longer. He overcame Army, grabbing two handfuls of the man's shirt. Army didn't pull away. "Stay, because I love you. If you can't believe anything I say, then look at me and see the truth."

Army's gaze moved over Brit's face, as if seeking the answers he needed. "I bought you beer."

A snort escaped Brit. He couldn't help it. "The legal drinking age in England is eighteen, so—in a way—you weren't completely wrong."

The small smile touching Army's lips gave Brit hope. "I can't believe I fell for a nineteen-year-old." He swiped a hand over his face. "Oh, god. I just realized you had a birthday while staying with me. I fell for an eighteen-year-old who only recently turned nineteen."

Despite the situation, a laugh escaped Brit. Still, he didn't release Army. The bloke was a runner. "It was inevitable. You're a librarian who loves books—old and new. I've been a theater actor since I was seven. We were meant to be."

Army dropped his hands and met Brit's stare. "Are you serious?"

Brit nodded. "I'm quite sought after at the Royal Exchange, you know. I've done more than two hundred appearances in my years on stage."

"Already?" Army asked, sounding blown away.

Brit warmed to the topic now that he could finally be honest. "I had private tutors in my downtime and finished school by fifteen." A sharp pang of loss hit Brit. There was no hiding it from his voice. "I thought I knew exactly where I was headed until Tanner called. When I dropped everything to come here, I never expected my life would become his. The things we do for family, I suppose." He smoothed his palms down Army's chest.

Army stared at him, wearing a solemn expression. "I think I'd like to kiss the real Brit for once."

Brit's mouth went dry. "Even though he's only nineteen?"

The space between them disappeared. Army's arms wrapped around Brit's waist. His smile bordered on wicked. "Especially since he's nineteen," Army said, lowering his head. Brit met him halfway. Their lips brushed. Army somehow managed to shift even closer. He grabbed Brit's ass and hauled him against his body as he deepened their kiss. Army dominated Brit, as always. "Goddamn," Army growled between kisses. "There's the man I love."

Brit's heart squeezed in his chest. Army wasn't finished with him yet. There was hope. Army held tight to Brit's jaw while he licked and nipped at Brit's mouth. As par for course, Brit could only hang on for the ride.

"Bloody hell, mate. This is by far the hottest kiss I've ever seen. You lucky wanker."

At Tanner's appearance, Brit buried his face against Army's throat to hide his blush. The way Army kept his arms wrapped around him warmed Brit's heart.

"I feel we should be properly introduced," Tanner said, as if he hadn't interrupted an intimate moment.

Brit turned his head while still clinging to Army. "I feel you should wait until later."

Tanner dropped the hand he'd extended for Army to shake. "Um. Yeah. That's probably best. I'll just..." He shuffled toward the door. "...find something else to do."

Brit held tight to Army, in case he thought to get away. He also kept his gaze locked on Tanner, ensuring the man really left them alone.

Army kissed the shell of his ear. "When will you go home?"

A new pain hit Brit's chest. His hold automatically tightened on Army. He couldn't lose this man. "That depends."

"On?"

"You," Brit answered honestly. "If you don't want me, I'll head home."

"And if I do want you?" Army asked, his expression gave nothing away. "Does that mean I'll be the new reason you don't get to live your dream?"

A smile tugged at the corners of Brit's mouth, and he shook his head. "Where do you think home is?"

"I'm assuming some place in England, and—well—you know my financial situation. It's not like I could afford to go see you there, but I'll be damned if I'm the reason you're not back on stage."

The more Army said, the bigger Brit's grin grew. He loved this man. "First off, I thought my home was with you. I can't imagine going from living like we're married to pretending the past four months didn't happen. As it is, I haven't slept more than three hours a night without you. Secondly, even if you decide you're done, I live in Atlanta." He paused. "Well, I guess—technically—I *lived* in Atlanta, and now I'm homeless. My lease was in Tanner's name, but there was some nonsense about the contract stating the apartment couldn't be unoccupied, so he let it go when we realized this body double thing would take longer than anticipated. I'm rambling again. Why are you the only person on the planet who makes me babble on like a complete prat?"

Army's smile made the confession worthwhile. "It's adorable. Keep going."

"That was it, really. I lived in Atlanta before this, working with the Shakespeare Company. I suppose I'm homeless now if you don't want me. The more I think about it, I feel kind of sick at the thought of ever going back to Atlanta."

Army sat back down.

A spike of fear ran through Brit. "Are you okay?"

Army met his gaze, looking lost. "I had this whole speech in my head when I came here about how I know you. I mean, I thought your birthday was in June and you were twenty-six, but I know you. When I walked through the door, it was on the tip of my tongue to tell you I know all the important things —like how you taste and what your skin smells like when we make love. All the things you can't fake. Instead, what left my mouth was that you're a complete stranger to me." Army's voice cracked on the last word, breaking Brit's heart. He cleared his throat. "I really just want to go home, climb in our bed, and forget the last three weeks ever happened, because—yes—I fucking want you." He shook his head. "But I don't know how to get there from here, Brit."

Brit squatted down between Army's knees. "Give me your keys."

An uncomfortable-sounding chuckle escaped Army. "Why? Are you calling in your loan?"

"The car was a gift. Give me your keys."

Army handed them over.

Brit's fingers closed around them. He traded Army for the set by handing the man his phone. "Here. Take this. If you don't know the way home, I do. While I drive, you can scroll through my photos, pepper me with questions, and search my name online. You can cyber stalk me and learn all about me. When we make it back to our little town no one has ever heard of, you'll learn on the job. Just as I had to do when I first moved in with you."

Army stared at Brit for so long Brit feared he was about to get shut down. Finally, Army turned the phone Brit's way. "You'll have to unlock this if I'm going to do all that."

It was hard work swallowing down his triumph, but Brit managed it. "The code is 755600. You'll need that in the future." As he pushed to his feet, Brit pressed a quick kiss to Army's lips before rushing to grab his bag. He wanted to be on the road before Army found anything about him he couldn't live with. All he had to do was make it home. Once he was instilled in Army's bed again, Army was never getting rid of him.

TWENTY MINUTES into their drive home, Brit couldn't take it any longer. "Are you okay over there?"

"Sort of thinking about leaping from the car," Army said, sounding unsure. "Your hair is a lot darker in these images of you online."

With his gaze locked on the road, Brit nodded. "I had to dye it to match Tanner's."

He could feel Army's stare boring into the side of his face. "You've been with me for months. How have I not noticed that?"

Brit shrugged. "You work all day. My stylist travels. He always came while you were at work." Being honest was a calculated risk. Brit needed Army to see him telling the truth. No matter how many past lies it revealed.

Army didn't rage. Instead, he went back to scrolling through Brit's phone. "I can't believe you do ballet. Please tell me you still have some of these tights. That's sexy as hell."

Brit bit the inside of his cheek to keep from smiling like an idiot. "I'm sure I have a pair somewhere. You still haven't explained why you're considering jumping from a moving car."

He saw Army shrug from the corner of his eye. "I can't compete with this, Brit. For fuck's sake, your dad is Euan Murray. I grew up listening to his music. You were born in Los Angeles before your dad took you to Keston, London, and you have a dual citizenship. It would take me all day to put together a list of the places you've lived and performed. Every new thing I learn about you puts you farther out of my reach. Hell, you might be even more out of my league than Tanner."

A snort escaped Brit before he could call it back. "Well, that's complete bullshit." Brit took advantage of having Army trapped. "I'm in love with you. You get that, right?" Brit said, glancing over and holding Army's gaze for a moment. "Nothing and no one can compete with you, because you own me. Why are you having such a hard time grasping that? Maybe I couldn't tell you I'm not Tanner, but I know for a fact I showed you every day that you are everything to me." Silence filled the car in the wake of Brit's rant. Brit fought the urge to look Army's way again. He couldn't force the man to forgive him or accept to him for himself.

"In a way, I feel like I lied to you too," Army said, making Brit's stomach cramp with dread. "When Tanner showed up, and I realized what you'd done, I was relieved."

Brit's throat threatened to swell closed. He tightened his grip on the wheel. "Why? We're you glad to be rid of me?"

"No," Army said so quickly and fiercely there could be no doubt he told the truth. "I was glad the Brit Murray I'd separated in my mind from Tanner was a real person. Every time I thought about you going back to filming or working conventions—to being Tanner, you stopped feeling real to me. I wanted..." Army paused and started over. "I want a real life with you. It wasn't an option with Tanner. All the times I pretended I could let you leave me, I lied to you and to myself. I had a whole other plan in mind for us."

Brit was too scared to hope. "What plan?"

Army brushed his fingers through Brit's hair. "I wish I'd been brave enough to go through with my plans for you on Valentine's Day," Army said instead of answering.

"Valentine's Day was awesome," Brit said, flashing Army a smile.

Army looked entirely too serious for Brit's comfort. "It was," he agreed. "But it might've been even better if I'd had the courage to ask you to marry me like I planned to do."

Brit stared at the road and fought not to react. He wanted to jerk the wheel, steering to the side of the road so he could capture Army's lips. They needed cool heads and rational thinking right now. Before they got home, Brit wanted all the air cleared so he could hold Army with no more secrets between them. He cleared his throat. "In a way, I'm glad you didn't ask. If you had, I would've had to say no, because it wouldn't have been me you were asking, but Tanner."

"Oh," Army said, sounding hurt. "Then I guess it's a good thing I—"

"But if you were to ask me now," Brit said, interrupting. "I'd probably wreck in my hurried attempt to get us home, so I could make love to my soon-to-be husband."

"I didn't know then that you're only nineteen. Maybe I should wait until you've had time to figure out if you're settling with me."

Army's response cut through Brit's heart like the sharpest blade. He tried swallowing the bitterness, hoping it wouldn't show in his voice. "Do you know how old I feel? Probably closer to fifty," he answered without giving Army time to guess. "I've been working nonstop since I was seven and I've lived alone since I was fourteen. My mom traded me to my dad for a price I've never been told. All I know is she was thrilled to learn she'd be set for life when she found out she was pregnant with a celebrity's baby, but less than thrilled to be pregnant with me. My dad thinks money equates love and replaces his presence. He pumps my account full of money, and—to him—that's all I need in life. I guess, in a way, he's been right. I had a driver to take me to rehearsals, shows, and to the next audition. Tanner taught me how to drive and brought me to the US when he moved here. My life has been work and watching my only real family member slowly disappear, becoming an addict and nothing else. I'm a tired old man in a young body." Brit signaled his lane change before getting off at the next exit. He didn't say anything else, nor did he want to. They needed gas if they planned to make the final thirty-minute drive of their trip.

He watched the numbers tick by on the pump while trying to cool his temper. Army was hung up on age. Seriously? Of all fucking things. Brit wanted to beat his head against a wall. He didn't know how much more he could take of life kicking him. His brain itched inside his head, making Brit want to scream. Army had planned to propose. Jesus, the longing in Brit's gut was crippling. Army had been on the verge of offering Brit the home he'd never had, and he'd changed his mind. Brit shoved his hands in his pockets to keep from punching out the window of

Army's car. Every move he made was exaggerated. He slammed the gas nozzle back in its place before tightening the cap until his hand cramped. His footsteps slapped the ground as he stormed back to the driver's side. Brit took a deep breath before opening the door. It wasn't Army's fault Brit craved more than he'd ever have. When he climbed behind the wheel, Army turned sideways in his seat.

He held a ring out. "Will you marry me?"

Brit blinked. He stopped breathing. It was a gorgeous gold band with three small diamonds sunk inside the gold. Considering how Army struggled for every dime, it must've taken everything for him to pay the ring. "You brought it with you."

Army didn't drop his arm. "I've taken it everywhere with me since I bought it, hoping I'd have a burst of courage. If you want to say no, I won't be angry. It's not like everything has been amazing the past few weeks. If nothing else, maybe this bullshit has proven that—no matter what—we'll be okay. I might not be in your league, but I love you more than anyone else ever could."

Brit heard the love and honesty in Army's every word. The rest of his life stared him in the face. He'd never known more hope and love. Brit was also scared as hell Army was only doing this to prove a point.

Army held his breath and the ring without letting up. He knew there was a real possibility Brit would turn him down. If he did, Army would accept Brit's answer. He wanted to spend the rest of his life with Brit, but he equally needed to prove there was nothing he'd learned since Tanner turned up in their lives that was enough to drive Army away. When he'd fallen for Brit, he'd fallen for Brit—not Tanner nor the idea of Tanner. He loved the man who wanted a Christmas tree and rarely let Army sleep from staring at him. Brit's past and age—everything was secondary to the way Brit made him feel. Tanner hadn't done that.

Brit eyed the ring. "Why are you doing this now? I don't want you to do this only because you think it's what I want."

The mistrust in Brit's voice hurt Army's chest. "This

is because I love you, and as much as I wish I could've made my proposal a grand moment for you, the truth is I don't have much else to offer other than my heart."

"Then, yes," Brit said, snagging the ring and putting it on. There was no happy celebration or kisses. Brit accepted and started the car.

Army stared at the man's profile with his bottom lip held between his teeth. He wanted to laugh. Brit truly was an old man in a young body. Laughter won. It bubbled in his throat before escaping. The way Brit's cheek curved let Army know the man was smiling.

"I love it when you're happy."

Army's smile grew even brighter at Brit's confession. "I love you."

Brit reached over and grabbed Army's hand before bringing it to his lips. He held it there. Army felt the man's breath catch against his skin.

"Are you okay?"

Brit nodded. Still, he kept his lips pressed to the back of Army's hand. "I thought I'd lost you." Brit's voice came out in a harsh whisper—like he was on the verge of tears. "The idea almost killed me."

Tears burned the backs of Army's eyes. He got it. In some freak series of events, they'd found each other. Army couldn't imagine ever being with anyone else. "I don't think it's possible for you to lose me. I think it's more likely I'd lose me before I could endure losing you." He knew he didn't make sense, but he'd spoken from the heart. Just the thought of never seeing Brit again made Army feel the insanity blossoming.

Brit glanced over for a second and caught Army's gaze. "I swear I'll never put anyone else above you again. Tanner has already been told I won't rescue him next time."

"Let's just get home, sexy. I'm ready to hold you until you beg me to give you peace."

Army wasn't sure if even then he'd let Brit go. The past few weeks had been hell. Their bed had been his prison. It was the only place that still held Brit's scent. Army had forced himself from it each day to work and nothing else. Now his gorgeous man would be there again. It was funny how little the lies mattered to Army's heart. It was frightening how much Army would endure to keep Brit. Maybe one day Brit would go too far or choose to walk away. Until then, Army planned to hang on through good times and bad, because he'd never met anyone more worthwhile.

Chapter Seven

It TURNED out the kitchen table Brit had bought them a while back was the sturdiest fucking table on the planet. The wooden piece held not only their half-finished dinner, flowers, and candles, but also a deliciously nude Brit. Army had given up trying to focus on eating his dinner almost half an hour earlier in favor of feasting on his gorgeous husband. He had no idea why Brit returning to his natural light brown hair and dark blue eyes was such a fucking turn-on, but Army could barely stand the shortest periods of staring at the man without attacking him. Army wasn't even one hundred percent certain how Brit had gone from sitting across from him to sprawled out for Army's oral enjoyment.

"Goddamn, I love you," Army growled for the hundredth time since the first brush of his tongue against Brit's hard cock.

Army palmed his erection through his jeans, trying to relieve the pressure. He was dying to get inside Brit, but he couldn't stop teasing the man into insanity. All this sexiness belonged to him. He needed to worship him.

"Love you too," Brit said, sounding hoarse.

Army came to his feet. As if the bottom half of Brit's body wasn't soaked in pre-cum and saliva, Army poured oil from the dressing bottle all over Brit's dick, balls, and asshole. He used his hands and fingers, ensuring everything had a good coating of lubricant, because he didn't intend to take it easy.

"I hope you're not allergic to whatever oil this is."

Brit clung to the edges of the kitchen table, panting and gasping. "Who fucking cares at this point? Just fuck me. I need you inside me—hard."

Army fingered Brit's ass while staring at the man's open desperation. He'd never felt more powerful. "Do you want to hear something funny?"

"No," Brit growled, sounding frustrated. "I want you to fuck me."

A chuckle that sounded evil even to Army's ears escaped him as he set his erection free. His eyes fell closed as he massaged his hard cock. "Mhmm. Did you know, before you, I'd never been a top? I was always the one who got fucked. But I kissed you that first time, and possessiveness took hold like I'd never felt before. I needed inside this sexy ass." Army probed Brit's asshole, teasing him.

A crazed-sounding laugh escaped Brit, even as he audibly sucked air. "You want to know something even funnier than that? I'd never been with a man at all before you. Not even a kiss."

Army froze with barely the tip of his cock inside his sexy husband. "Are you being serious?"

Another hysterical laugh filled the air. "You were the first person to ever make me hot—like my skin would fry from my body. That goes for men and women. Life was muted before you."

The possessiveness Army experienced the first time they kissed didn't hold a candle to the greed that overtook him in that moment. While holding Brit's stare, Army hooked his arms beneath the man's thighs and hauled his ass even closer and thrust deep. Their skin slapped as Army slammed against Brit's ass over and over again. No one else had ever touched his husband like this. Army was the only person to ever make Brit cry out the way he did now. That knowledge gripped hold of every molecule of Army. This gorgeous man was his and no one else's. He would make Brit happy and keep him screaming his name until death parted them, just as he'd promised in their wedding vows.

About the Author

Charity Parkerson is an award-winning and multi-published author with several companies. Born with no filter from her brain to her mouth, she decided to take this odd quirk and insert it in her characters.

*Eight-time Readers' Favorite Award Winner

*2015 Passionate Plume Award Finalist

*2013 Reviewers' Choice Award Winner

*2012 ARRA Finalist for Favorite Paranormal Romance

*Five-time winner of The Mistress of the Darkpath

Connect with her online:

*Sign up for her newsletter: https://sendfox.com/charityparkerson

*Join her readers' group on Facebook: http://bit.ly/CharitysTribe

*Website: https://www.charityparkerson.com

*A list of her social media accounts and giveaways all in one place: http://hy.page/charityparkerson